In the Eye
of War

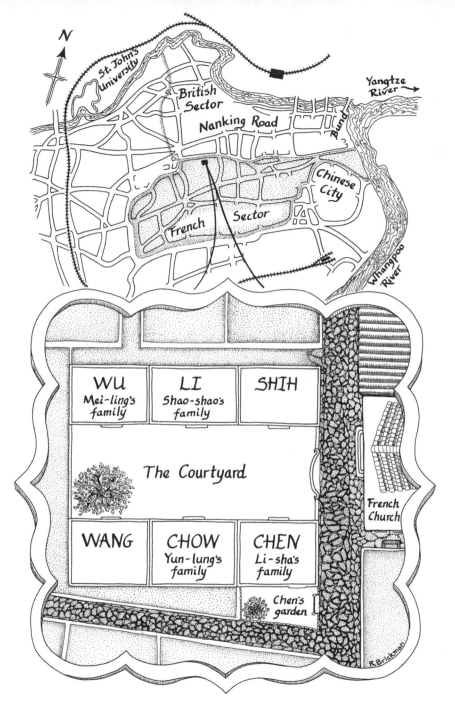

Top: Map of Shanghai showing the house where Shao-shao lives
Bottom: Drawing of the courtyard

Map by Robin Brickman

In the Eye of War

Margaret and Raymond Chang

MARGARET K. MCELDERRY BOOKS
NEW YORK

Margaret K. McElderry Books
Macmillan Publishing Company
866 Third Avenue
New York, New York 10022
Collier Macmillan Canada, Inc.
Designed by Barbara A. Fitzsimmons
First Edition
Printed in the United States of America
10 9 8 7 6 5 4 3 2 1
Library of Congress Cataloging-in-Publication Data
Chang, Margaret Scrogin.
In the eye of war / Margaret and Raymond Chang. — 1st ed.
p. cm.
Summary: During the final days of the Japanese occupation of
China, Shao-shao celebrates his tenth birthday, observes traditional
holidays with his family, and befriends the daughter of a traitor.
[1. Family life—Fiction.   2. China—History—1937–1945—Fiction.
3. World War, 1939–1945—Fiction.]   I. Chang, Raymond.   II. Title.
PZ7.C359667Ci   1990   [Fic]—dc20   89–38027 CIP   AC
ISBN 0-689-50503-5

*In Memory of Fourth Sister
and to
Elizabeth Hope:
May she never live in a world at war.*

Contents

City in the Eye of War   **1**

1   Games in the Sun   3
August 1944

2   Right Purpose   12
September 1944

3   Double Ten Day   24
October 10, 1944

4   Cocoons Burst   38
October 1944

5   Long Life   52
November 1944

6   Sunday Expedition   67
December 1944

7   The Year of the Cock   80
December 1944 – February 1945

8   The Bird   98
March 1945

9   **An Act of Charity**   **111**
April 1945

10   **A Wind for Kites**   **121**
April 1945

11   **Cricket Songs**   **132**
May 1945

12   **A Wish Granted**   **142**
May – July 1945

13   **Air Raids**   **154**
July 1945

14   **Blue Sky, White Sun**   **168**
August 1945

15   **A Cup of Tea**   **185**
August 1945

In the Eye of War

City in the Eye of War

IN THE CENTER OF EVERY HURRICANE there is a still, windless place called the eye.

The battlestorms that preceded World War II hit China first, when the Japanese invaded Manchuria in 1931. Within two years, they had occupied four of China's northern provinces, and in 1937 sent invasion troops south. Chiang Kai-shek's Nationalist Party governed China then, and Chiang's capital, Nanking, suffered most from the invading Japanese. Chiang and other civilian and military leaders escaped to Chungking, far inland up the Yangtze River.

Shanghai, a great city at the mouth of the Yangtze, had been ruled by Europeans for more than a century. The British and French each owned a sector of the city, where they could build their own houses, choose their own leaders, and make their own laws. Before World War II, European and Chinese businessmen got rich by shipping Chinese goods out of Shanghai to the rest of the world. When the Japanese invaded, Chinese soldiers defended the countryside around the port city, but the foreigners, hoping to continue business as usual, surrendered peacefully. Japanese soldiers did not destroy Shanghai or slaughter its people, as they did in Nanking.

Meanwhile, in 1939 Hitler's Germany went to war in Europe, invading Poland and France. The Japanese Empire joined Germany and, in December 1941, asserted its supremacy in the Pacific Ocean by bombing the American naval base at Pearl Harbor in the Hawaiian Islands. The United States, Britain, Free France, and China now had a common enemy.

As the war continued, Japanese occupation troops took English and American citizens from their homes in Shanghai to internment camps outside the city. Middle-class Chinese, neither very rich nor very poor, continued to live in the European sectors as they had before the war. They were comfortable, isolated from the calamities of war. They never ran out of rice.

Their lives were peaceful, there in the eye of war. Yet they knew the battlestorm could hit them any time.

1. Games in the Sun
August 1944

"MINE'S FEROCIOUS," BOASTED SHAO-shao.

"Mine's bigger," Yun-lung shot back.

Late afternoon sun baked the walls and cobble-stones of the courtyard. The boys crouched in the shade of a tree near Yun-lung's house, each holding a small clay pot. Across the courtyard, near its gate-way, a girl stood on her front steps and watched them. Except for her and the boys, the courtyard was empty.

Inside the pots were male crickets, both un-defeated after a summer of fights.

"If you're so sure of him, let them fight in my pot." Yun-lung set his pot on the hard earth between them.

"He can beat yours anywhere," Shao-shao replied.

The girl walked cautiously toward them.

Paying no attention to her, Shao-shao slid back the cover of his pot, slipped his hand inside, and grabbed his cricket. It moved its hard legs against his palm but did not bite. With one swift motion, he dropped it into Yun-lung's pot.

The boys peered down, their foreheads almost touching as they watched Shao-shao's cricket explore. The crickets had to find each other by touch. If you spent your whole life in the dark underground, Shao-shao thought, you wouldn't need to see.

"Ah," Yun-lung breathed. The crickets had brushed antennas. Immediately, both extended their fangs, tiny threads of ivory. The fight had begun.

Shyly, the girl came closer, peering at the crickets over Yun-lung's head. Shao-shao glanced up at her. She offered a quick, sweet smile. He looked down, pretending he had not noticed.

"Get him, get him." Yun-lung cheered his cricket on. Heavy, often clumsy, he rocked on his knees. Sweat made his short-cropped hair stand in spikes.

The crickets locked fangs and wrestled head to head, their slender legs braced against red clay.

"Hey, Li-sha, get lost," Yun-lung said to the girl, not bothering to glance back at her. Shao-shao saw her blink and tighten her lips. She circled to stand behind him.

"Fight, you can beat him." Shao-shao clenched his fists. His cricket was like him, small but agile. Shao-shao could beat Yun-lung in Ping-Pong anytime.

He wished he dared ask Li-sha to come closer and cheer for his cricket.

The crickets quivered. They were straining, fang against fang, each trying to knock the other off its feet.

Li-sha crouched down, her knees close together, her short skirt pulled tight across her legs.

Then the fight was over. Shao-shao's cricket flipped over, pulled back, and ran away as Yun-lung's chased him around the pot.

"Undefeated and still champion!" Yun-lung smiled and raised his fists in celebration. In the pot, his cricket chirped a victory song while Shao-shao's stood silent.

Li-sha made a soft sympathetic sound in her throat.

Shao-shao looked down at his knees, hearing a streetcar rumble along Nanking Road and Li-sha's baby brother cry. He knew his cricket might fight again before winter came. It might even win. But it would never have the same spirit.

The shrill whine of an air-raid siren drowned out Yun-lung's cries.

Li-sha sprang to her feet and dashed home.

Shao-shao stood up. His heartbeat shook his whole body.

Gao-ma ran out of Shao-shao's house, waving her arms, her mouth open. "Come in!" she called.

The siren hammered them with its wail. Shao-shao tried to keep his hand steady as he reached into Yun-lung's pot to take back his cricket. It would run away if he dropped it.

"Quick, quick," Gao-ma yelled, as Shao-shao covered his cricket pot. She pulled Yun-lung up by the collar. "Go home now." She shoved him toward his door.

"Hurry, hurry!" Gao-ma swept Shao-shao inside and slammed the door behind them.

She headed for the kitchen, where Ah-fong, their younger servant, would be hiding. She expected Shao-shao to follow her, for his parents and sisters were out. But he had already glimpsed Second Brother on the landing above, running upstairs toward the veranda. If he started now, he could be on the roof by the time the old servant caught her breath and came to look for him.

"Go back!" Second Brother shot an angry whisper down the stairs when he saw Shao-shao coming. "You'll get me in trouble!"

Though fear rattled through him like a string of exploding firecrackers, Shao-shao followed his older brother. He hitched himself up to perch on the veranda railing. Balancing three stories above the cement back court, he grasped the glazed tiles at the edge of the sloping roof, pushed off from the railing, hoisted himself up, and clambered along rows of curved tiles until he found a firm foothold. He knew his face and clothes would be dirty, but he did not care. He crouched, panting and sweating, the smell of warm roof tiles and damp green leaves heavy in his nostrils. He squinted into the bright sky, listening for the distant roar of American bombers.

The rooftops of Shanghai, wavering in the hazy, humid air, stretched around him in all directions. The steeple of the French church rose above the houses of his neighborhood; the trees along Nanking Road blocked his northern view. All over the city, people

6

would be out on the rooftops, where Japanese soldiers could not see them, watching for American bombers. Sometimes the Americans flew right over the city to bomb Japanese planes at the inland airfield. Sometimes they swept low over the Bund, the waterfront along the Whangpoo River, to destroy Japanese ships docked there. More often, formations of American bombers went high overhead, on their way to bomb Japan itself.

When he saw American planes in the daytime or heard them at night, Shao-shao liked to imagine the pilots in their cockpits. He had never seen an American, except in the movies. But he had heard about them from Teacher Bao, who once studied in America. Shao-shao had seen Englishmen when his family lived in Hong Kong. Americans looked like the English, with pale, puffy skin, rosy cheeks, and big noses. He thought the pilots would be laughing carelessly. They were not afraid of the Japanese. They flew right over Japanese guns, almost as if they were teasing.

"There!" shouted Second Brother, balancing on his knees, his broad, handsome face flushed with heat and excitement. Then Shao-shao saw the formation of six planes high in the sky, heading inland. Once more he clenched his fists, resting his knuckles against warm tiles.

From far away came the soft pop of Japanese antiaircraft guns. Curving lines of black smoke looped up into the sky, like ropes to pull down the planes. This time they couldn't catch one. With a triumphant roar, the bombers veered upward and out of sight.

"Looks like they went for Hungjao." Shading his eyes against the afternoon sun, Second Brother looked toward the airfield east of the city. An explosion growled like distant thunder. They watched silently for a while, until slow black clouds billowed up. Triumph surged in Shao-shao's heart. He thought of Japanese tanks and planes engulfed in flames, of Japanese soldiers killed.

"Come down from there this instant!" Gao-ma's shrill voice, their household's private air-raid siren, called from the veranda. "Stupid, silly boys," she scolded as they made their way down over the tiles. "Last week a boy got hit with shrapnel during an air raid." Braced firmly on her big feet, she helped Shao-shao down, her strong, coarse hands around his waist.

"I heard about it from their servant." She bent her head as if to make sure her words went directly into Shao-shao's ear. "He's crippled for life."

Second Brother jumped from the roof. Gao-ma turned her anger on him. "You should set an example for this one," she said. "Just wait till your parents get home."

"Oh, Gao-ma, I told him not to come. How can I help it if he follows me?"

Second Brother put his hands on the old woman's shoulders, smiling. If anyone could charm her out of her bad temper, he could. "Come on, Gao-ma, you won't tell on us? We promise not to do it again. Besides, you've gone up there yourself, I know you have."

Smoothing down Second Brother's hair, Gao-ma shook her head, laughing at her own foolishness. "If you really promise, and you, too, Shao-shao."

Both brothers nodded solemnly.

"Gao-ma, they hit Hungjao," Shao-shao said as they went into the dim house and down the stairs.

"Good for them." She put an arm around him. "Let's hope no innocent people were killed. Now go wash up. Your mother and father will be home soon, and I made dumplings for supper."

When Mother arrived about half an hour later, Shao-shao and Second Brother sat at the table in the family room, quietly playing chess as if nothing had happened. Shao-shao heard the door open and Mother's strong, rapid voice calling, "Gao-ma, is Mr. Li here? Where are the children?"

Shao-shao ran to the second-floor landing and leaned against the railing, as Mother, one hand on the banister and the other on Fourth Sister's shoulder, slowly mounted the stairs. She paused on the landing beside the door to the storage room, where the stairs made a turn.

Mother's feet had been bound when she was a small child living behind her father's shop. Everyone but peasants bound girls' feet in those days. The Republic was established and foot binding was outlawed before she grew up, so her feet were not as small as Grandmother's. But she still had trouble walking.

"Shao-shao!" she cried up the stairs. "Is your

brother here? Is Ah-fong in the house? Where is Third Sister?"

"I held Grandmother's hand," Fourth Sister announced, her bobbed hair swinging across her cheek. "She was afraid, but I wasn't. I told her the Americans wouldn't bomb us. They're our friends."

Second Brother leaned against the doorway of the family sitting room, his arms folded across his solid chest. "Third Sister's with that brainy friend of hers. Reviewing their notes from last year." He swung his head and rolled his eyes to show his contempt for his older sister, her friend, and their diligent studies.

Mother mounted the last step and stopped, horrified. "At Kuo Yuan-yi's? With all those Japs? She'll be lucky if she gets home at all. What did I do in my previous life to deserve this worry?"

Because of the air raid, Mother knew the Japanese would set up checkpoints between their house and Yuan-yi's street in the old British Sector, where no British lived. Early last year, the Japanese had sent them all to prison camps.

The telephone rang, startling them all. Second Brother ran to answer it. Mother gripped Shao-shao's shoulder with a slender white hand, her eyes intent on Second Brother, who spit grunts of one syllable into the black receiver.

"That's Third Sister," he announced. "She says to tell you she'll be home in about an hour."

"I thought it might be Father. He said he'd be at the Golden Dragon this afternoon, so he should be all right." Every day, Father went to meet his friends at the Golden Dragon restaurant.

Mother patted the smooth black bun at the nape of her neck, drew a deep breath, and looked at Shao-shao as if seeing him for the first time. She rummaged in her purse, pulled out an embroidered handkerchief, and wiped the dust from Shao-shao's face. The handkerchief smelled of sandalwood and her hand was cool and smooth against his forehead as she brushed back his hair. She collapsed in her chair by the window of the family sitting room and asked for tea in a weary voice.

"Did you find your mother well?" Gao-ma asked as she set the pink porcelain tea mug, with its design of flowers and bats for good luck, on the table beside Mother's chair. Mother lifted the lid of the mug and breathed in the jasmine fragrance.

"She is no worse. She frets too much about my brother." Mother sipped her tea, then put the mug down and leaned forward to look out the window. Shao-shao peered out, too. The courtyard was empty. Yun-lung's parents wouldn't let him come out again this evening.

"I hope she lives to see the end of this war," Mother said. "I hope we all do."

2. Right Purpose
September 1944

LI WU-JIANG, OR BOUNDLESS FUTURE, was the youngest in his family, so everyone called him Shao-shao, Little Brother. Sometimes he imagined himself standing at the bottom of a long flight of stairs, like those at the temple where Mother prayed, with his family lined up above him.

Fourth Sister would be one step up. On the step above her would stand Second Brother, and then Third Sister. The step above Third Sister would be empty, because Second Sister died before he was born. First Brother would stand above the empty step. The Japanese had taken him away to do hard labor, but he wrote them from time to time. Shao-shao didn't like to remember First Brother, so he skipped quickly to First Sister, eldest of the Li children, now married and living with her husband's family. Mother would stand above her, and then Father, the head of the family. Above him were the spirits of their ancestors, who watched over family fortunes.

In September, the four youngest Li children returned to school. They went six days a week, with Saturday a half day. Third Sister took the streetcar every morning to her classes at St. John's University on the eastern edge of the city, across Soochow Creek. Second Brother walked to Middle School. This year Fourth Sister went with him.

"Don't let Fourth Sister out of your sight," Mother ordered him. Shao-shao knew he obeyed, mostly because Fourth Sister would tell on him if he didn't. But when they walked, Second Brother and his friend Tak-ming, Yun-lung's older brother, lagged far behind Fourth Sister and her friend from next door, Wu Mei-ling.

Shao-shao and Yun-lung, starting their fifth year at the Right Purpose Elementary School, still had to walk to school with a servant. Gao-ma and Yun-lung's servant took turns. Shao-shao liked it best when Gao-ma went. She had been with his family since they first lived in Shanghai. When Father moved his business to Hong Kong after the Japanese started making trouble, she went along. She had taken care of Shao-shao when Mother brought him home from the hospital in Hong Kong. Fourth Sister always said he was Gao-ma's favorite. He knew that was true, though he would never say so out loud.

The two boys often passed Li-sha and her nursemaid on their way to school, but the boys never walked with her, nor did the servants speak to each other.

One morning late in September, Gao-ma lagged

behind Shao-shao and Yun-lung. The boys ran ahead around a corner and stopped dead when they saw Japanese soldiers at the end of the next block.

With their helmets, heavy boots, and bayonets mounted on their rifles, they looked like demon shadow puppets. They had blocked the road with sawhorses so they could question everyone who went by.

The boys could not turn back. If they did, the soldiers would think they were trying to escape and chase or shoot them. There was nothing to do but walk forward. Slowly. Gao-ma caught up with them and pushed them ahead, her hands on their shoulders. Like the other Chinese around him, Shao-shao kept his eyes on the sidewalk. He must not stare at the bayonets gleaming in the sun. Fear rose in his throat, choking him. They could shoot him or stab him with those bayonets. That was how they executed Chinese resistance fighters. He had seen pictures in the newspaper.

He dared not lift his head and look directly into the face beneath the helmet. If he did, he would be visible, be noticed. Then he would be in danger.

People stopped ahead of them. Gao-ma squeezed his shoulder, and he stood still. "They're questioning someone," she whispered.

Shao-shao heard a soldier barking out questions in Japanese while a Chinese collaborator translated. "Where do you live? Where are you going? Where do you work?" Shao-shao could not hear the answers,

14

for the young man, too, held his head down. He spoke softly, respectfully.

The line moved again. Step by step, they came closer to the soldiers. Shao-shao felt his breakfast porridge rise in his throat. He stared at the young man's feet, in heavy-soled cotton shoes, and the polished black boots of the soldiers. They wore thick leather belts around their waists. Ammunition bands crossed their chests. The Chinese man's knees bent slightly under his loose blue cotton trousers.

"Move along," another soldier ordered Gao-ma. Shao-shao's knees felt weak and trembly, but Gao-ma propelled him from behind so that he had to pass in front of the soldiers.

They did not run or talk until they had turned the corner, out of the soldiers' sight.

At the school gate, Gao-ma handed Shao-shao his schoolbag and told him to be good. A shrill whistle blew. The students milling around the school court-yard arranged themselves into straight lines, facing Teacher Hung. He stood on a platform in front of the school building, stocky and muscular in his white shirt and blue shorts. As he began their morning exercise routine, his whistle bounced against his chest.

Shao-shao slapped his hands together, then swung them wide as his feet jumped apart and together. He breathed in great lungfuls of air, wishing he could crush a soldier between his palms like a fly. Slowly, his stomach stopped quaking and his knees grew strong again. Beside him, Yun-lung moved heavily, off-rhythm. Shao-shao wondered if his friend had been scared, too, but he didn't dare ask.

The morning bell signaled the end of calisthenics. Everyone crowded into the school building.

Flushed and panting, the fifth-graders waited in their seats. Shao-shao stared at his own battered desk, at the wrinkled white blouse and long, black pigtails of Lian-di, the girl stuffed into the seat before him, at the empty blackboard. Li-sha sat in the first seat of the row to his left. She had glanced briefly at him when she took her seat, looking as if she wanted to smile. He had returned a brief nod, hoping no one else would notice.

Teacher Yang strode through the door, a thin, severe woman in dark brown silk, holding a sheaf of papers in her hand. She faced the class, unsmiling.

Everyone stood up and bowed. "Good morning, Teacher Yang," they said in unison.

"Good morning, students," she replied crisply. Signaling them to be seated, she passed out their papers.

Shao-shao breathed a sigh of relief when he saw his mark, but Pei-fu, the lanky boy in the seat next to him, was not so fortunate.

"Liu Pei-fu, your characters look like chicken scratches," Teacher Yang announced, punctuating her words with swings of a ruler. "You're a lazy boy who doesn't practice. Come up here."

Hanging his head, Pei-fu clumped along the row of desks until he stood facing the teacher. "Hold out your hand," she commanded.

16

Slowly, he turned his palm upward. Teacher smacked the ruler across his open hand.

He let out a soft breath, but did not cry. He came prepared, Shao-shao thought. He must have spread wax over his palm.

Shao-shao did not watch Pei-fu return to his seat. Like everyone else, he was busy searching his schoolbag for his ink stick, ink stone, brushes, paper, and exercise books. Teacher Yang started the water jug on its journey from student to student. They had been working on the opening couplet of the "Three-Character Classic."

Teacher wrote the words they had already practiced on the board, reciting, "Men at birth are naturally . . ."

She turned to the class. "Today we practice the last word." On the board, she completed the sentence, writing the character for "good." "Page twenty-one in your copybooks," she reminded them.

Shao-shao poured a little water into the shallow well in his ink stone and rubbed his ink stick in it until he had rich black ink. Carefully, he placed his tracing paper over his copybook, matching up the grid of lines that enclosed the repeated character, dipped his brush in ink, and traced "good."

There were a lot of small lines, and his hand kept trembling. The first few characters he wrote looked weak and fleshy, but he was not discouraged. He knew he must forget the soldiers and focus his mind on each stroke.

"Concentrate," Father had told him, when he was

seven and just beginning to learn calligraphy. He remembered Father, tall and erect in a chair beside him, showing him the proper way to sit. "Keep your spine straight," Father had said. "The brush must be straight. Grip it firmly. Concentrate."

Shao-shao felt his body relax, his mind grow calmer. At last he put aside the copybook and tracing paper, smoothed a fresh sheet of calligraphy paper over his desk, and began to write freehand.

Father always said that a man's character was revealed in his handwriting. "You're fortunate to go to school, to learn calligraphy properly," he had told Shao-shao more than once. "I had to teach myself." Although Father's calligraphy was not as neat as Mother's, it was better, because it was strong and alive.

Shao-shao paused to look at the page he had nearly filled. "You learn quickly when you put your mind to it," Father had told him. He tried hard to write carefully yet keep the spontaneity that marked good calligraphy. He filled his brush at the ink stone and began to form the square, the open mouth at the bottom of the character "good."

A huge blob of ink splattered across his paper.

Lian-di's pigtail swung over his ink stone and sent ink flying across his calligraphy.

Shao-shao let out a cry of rage, grabbed the pigtail, and pulled as hard as he could. The picture of a thrusting bayonet flashed into his mind.

Lian-di screamed. Teacher Yang pointed her ruler and demanded an explanation.

18

Like everyone in the front rows, Li-sha turned and stared, shocked.

Lian-di began to blubber, like a stupid girl. "He pulled my braid," she said.

"Li Wu-jiang, come up here." The class fell silent as Teacher Yang called Shao-shao's name.

She gave Shao-shao three strokes with the ruler and made him stand in the corner near the blackboard while she told the class how naughty he was. He stood there for the rest of the period, listening to suppressed snickers, curling and uncurling his stinging hand.

He said nothing to Lian-di when he returned to his seat for math class. What was there to say? He slammed the beads of his abacus savagely. The clatter of thirty abacuses seemed to match his mood. At least she kept her braids flipped forward.

He hoped her head still hurt.

When the noon bell rang, Shao-shao and Yun-lung joined the mass of students jostling and shouting their way downstairs to the courtyard for noon recess. The boys did not go home for lunch, as many of their classmates did. Gao-ma or Yun-lung's servant brought lunch to them, steaming hot from home in a fitted stack of round metal trays. Side by side on a wooden bench, the boys compared lunches. The first tray always held rice. For Shao-shao, Gao-ma had packed fried bean curd and Chinese cabbage left over from the night before. Yun-lung had spicy bean curd. The faster they ate, the sooner they could run to the first floor hallway and claim a Ping-Pong table.

The first class after lunch was history, taught by Teacher Yu, a tall, ungainly young man with a limp and a shock of hair that never lay flat. He quizzed them on their reading about the short Yuan Dynasty, when Mongols from the north ruled China.

"Chen Li-sha, when did the Yuan Dynasty begin?"

"1279."

Shao-shao liked the sweet, musical sound of Li-sha's voice, but he knew he should not talk to her. His parents had warned him to be careful what he said in Yun-lung's house, because the Chows shared a wall with Li-sha's house, and her father was a collaborator with the Japanese.

Teacher Yu asked, "Soong Pei-fu, who was the second emperor of the Yuan Dynasty?"

"Yuan Chen."

Correct answers, question after question. Shao-shao contributed the date, 1368, when Chu Yuan-chang threw off the Mongol yoke and founded the Ming Dynasty.

"Congratulations." Teacher Yu smiled broadly. "You studied hard last night. To reward you, I won't ask any more questions. Instead, I'll tell you a story you won't find in your history books. It's about the fall of the Yuan Dynasty."

A pleased sigh echoed all over the classroom. Everyone settled back to listen.

"First you must know that most of the Mongol barbarians could not read or write. They knew the people hated them and they passed many harsh laws to prevent uprisings. They even made their Chinese subjects give up kitchen knives for fear that they might be used as weapons."

Shao-shao tried to imagine what Gao-ma and Mother would do without knives. Would they have to give up eating with chopsticks and tear at food with their teeth, like animals?

"Since everyone hated them, the tyrants could not last long. Brave Chinese leaders planned a rebellion. They gathered weapons. All over the country, people joined the plot. How could so many people know exactly when to rise up? There were no printing presses, no newspapers, no radios."

Shao-shao wondered how they dared to fight so strong an enemy. Mongol swords must have been as sharp as bayonets.

"They found a way," Teacher Yu continued. "They decided to invent a new custom. At the harvest moon festival in the middle of August, they passed out small, round cakes shaped like the full moon. On the same night in cities and villages of all the nearby provinces, people broke open these cakes to eat them. Inside each cake, there was a slip of paper on which was written, 'Death to all Mongols on August fifteenth.' It was perfect. Even if a Mongol soldier got his hands on one, he couldn't read the message. So on August fifteenth, the people rebelled spontaneously, all together, all at once. The Yuan Dynasty crumbled overnight. You see, when the people unite, no one can stop them. So we eat moon cakes on August fifteenth to celebrate their bravery."

Shao-shao kept thinking about moon cakes as Teacher Bao led them through their English lesson. "A is for Apple, B is for Boy, C is for Cat," they chanted. Because Teacher Bao had studied in America, he always wore Western suits with a bow tie and oiled his hair so it would wave up from a part, like Clark Gable's in *Gone With the Wind.*

If every Chinese rebelled, all at once, united, could they defeat the Japanese, as they had once defeated the Mongols? Shao-shao didn't think so. That was just a story, and anyway it happened six hundred years ago.

"Good-bye, my friends, good-bye my friends. See you tomorrow," Shao-shao sang with his class, and school was over for another day, a separate world he left behind when he passed through the school gateway.

After school, when Shao-shao and Yun-lung were together, they were allowed to go home without a servant. They never knew when they might have to stay for soccer or Ping-Pong practice. Anyway, the women were busy preparing supper. The boys were grateful for the freedom.

That afternoon they wandered through the streets of the French Sector. The Japanese soldiers had left, and people on the streets relaxed, enjoying the late-afternoon sunshine.

They stopped at the music shop, where Shao-shao tried out a harmonica, and at the store off Nanking Road that sold comic books and silkworms. They had bought their first silkworms before school started, when they were tiny mites, newly hatched, no bigger than the tip of a pencil. They both wanted a few more.

Shao-shao's father did not approve of pets. He only allowed the cats because they caught mice and because Mother liked them. He didn't want to spend good money on food for useless animals, he always said, and the house was crowded enough with four children, Gao-ma, and Ah-fong. Shao-shao had to be satisfied with crickets and silkworms as pets. He kept them in his room, where Father could not see them.

"How many would you like?" the old shopkeeper asked, as the boys examined the wide metal trays, filled with wriggling silkworms chewing mulberry leaves. By now, the largest silkworms were half as long as a pencil.

Yun-lung and Shao-shao each had enough money to buy five silkworms and a bundle of mulberry leaves. Shao-shao selected the fattest, liveliest silkworms he could find. They felt smooth and tender between his fingers and tickled as they crawled across his palm. They would need lots of food to prepare them for the coming months, when they would sleep inside their silk cocoons, turning into moths.

Loaded down with schoolbags, boxes of silkworms, and bundles of mulberry leaves, the boys headed straight home. In the lingering summer twilight, they still had time for a game of marbles before dark.

3. Double Ten Day
October 10, 1944

MOTHER'S CALL BARELY ROUSED SHAO-shao. Second Brother turned and groaned in his bed across the room. Third Sister scolded through the door, but still the boys did not leave their beds.

Shao-shao had stayed up late reading a kung-fu novel, since Father was at the Golden Dragon with his former business partners. Before the war, they had sold cloth all over China. Now Shao-shao was pretty sure they smuggled cloth inland to the Chinese army, but he was not supposed to know anything about that. When Shao-shao fell asleep, he knew Third Sister, Second Brother, and Mother were still watching for Father.

"Come down here! You'll all be late for school!" Father's angry voice jerked Shao-shao upright. Second Brother dived for his school uniform.

"Father's back!" Shao-shao cried. He fumbled for his pants draped over the foot of his bed.

Shao-shao heard Fourth Sister's feet on the stairs.

24

"The boys aren't dressed yet," she yelled, so all the household could hear.

"He got back after midnight." Second Brother looked in the mirror as he buttoned his jacket, then dramatically turned on his heel, his hand a revolver aimed at Shao-shao. "The Japs stopped him and his friends outside the restaurant. Asked them a lot of questions." He screwed his face into a menacing expression, playing the role of a soldier. *"Hai! Anyeto wing-woo des ca?"*

Two years of compulsory Japanese lessons had taught him how to parody the language he hated.

Shao-shao pulled on his shirt, remembering the poor young man he had seen at the Japanese road-block several weeks ago.

"They used all their money to bribe the translator," Second Brother went on, reveling in the tale of disaster. "Then it took them a long time to find a pedicab. The driver had to wait while Father came in to get more money."

An angry roar sounded up the stairs: "Where are you?"

Second Brother lifted his schoolbag and started downstairs. "You'd better hurry or you'll be in big trouble," he said. Shao-shao followed him, trying to button his jacket as he ran downstairs.

But Father did not even notice that Shao-shao slipped into the last empty seat at the breakfast table.

He's angry about something else, Shao-shao thought. Irritation dominated Father's full, handsome face, drawing the thick brows together, tensing

25

the muscles of his jaw. His lips, below his stylish mustache, were pursed as if he'd eaten poison. He glared at the bowl before him.

"Is this all we have to go with the porridge?" he scolded Mother. "Only two dishes!"

Shao-shao looked at the two varieties of pickled vegetables Ah-fong had placed on the table. He hated both kinds, and he knew his brothers and sisters did, too. But he said nothing. When Father was in a mood like this, the best thing was to mind your own business and keep silent.

"That's all Gao-ma could buy this week," Mother said softly.

"You mean you didn't give the grocer his extra. You know very well there's plenty of food in Shanghai, if you've got enough cash."

Mother ate a tiny morsel of pickled cabbage. Shao-shao noticed that her hand, holding her chopsticks, trembled slightly. "Fat Ming's sure to have something better next time he comes," she said.

Fat Ming had been bringing them food ever since they moved to Shanghai. Shao-shao knew, without knowing how he knew, that this food was a reward for Father's secret services to the Chinese army.

"That Chen fellow's eating duck's eggs and beef, you can be sure of that." Father tossed his head, pointing his chin in the direction of Li-sha's house. "He never did coolie work for his rice. All that stuff he had moved in! And three servants! Making money hand over fist building roads for the Japs. Filthy collaborator!"

26

Shao-shao remembered the day last summer when Li-sha arrived. A line of porters carried baskets and bags, trunks and boxes, antique chests, a new mahogany dining table, rosewood beds with new mattresses, two birds in a cage. He had hoped that Li-sha would bring the birds out for air so he could get a closer look at them. But she never did. Less than a week after she arrived, Father told him he must stay away from the Chens. Mr. Chen worked for the Japanese.

"He has good food, but in his heart he knows he's betraying his country." Third Sister tossed one long braid over her shoulder. "Especially today."

She was speaking of the holiday they could not celebrate, the tenth day of the tenth month, the anniversary of the revolution that toppled the Manchu Dynasty and established the Republic. The people of Shanghai were supposed to be loyal subjects of the Japanese Emperor Hirohito now. The Republic was Hirohito's enemy.

Shao-shao had seen the Emperor in newsreels, festooned with medals, wearing white gloves, erect on his big white horse. Rows and rows of Japanese soldiers marched before him. Bayonets bristled, and the Japanese flag, a rising sun, billowed in the wind.

Father spooned a large portion of pickled vegetables over his porridge, ate a few bites, wiped his mouth, then answered Third Sister quietly.

"You're right. At least we haven't bought our rice by working for our enemies."

Third Sister leaned forward, her eyes shining. "Oh, no. We can be proud of—"

"Quiet!" Mother whispered sharply, shaking her head.

Everyone looked down at the table, pretending not to hear. Shao-shao knew that when Fat Ming brought them food, he sometimes gave Father papers, papers Shao-shao was not supposed to see.

Father likes Third Sister to admire him, Shao-shao thought. His throat relaxed. He swallowed a big spoonful of pickled vegetables. They tasted sour, but he knew better than to upset everyone by complaining now that Third Sister had managed to soothe Father. Father listened to Third Sister because he was proud of her achievements. She had been accepted at St. John's University. She studied hard and earned good marks.

Father rapped his porridge bowl against his plate and set down his chopsticks. He said to Mother, more sad now than angry, "It's the worst Double Ten Day I can remember. The Japs have the whole coast, now they've taken Foochow. The Americans will never be able to land."

"It still seems strange that we're all going to school on Double Ten Day." Third Sister pushed her porridge bowl away.

"Even worse, Stringbean Kamakura's giving a test in Japanese," Second Brother said.

"Just wait till you have to learn Japanese," Fourth Sister told Shao-shao. "You'll hate it."

The bright autumn day, with its blue sky and warm dry breeze, made Shao-shao long for school to end.

Not one of the teachers dared mention Double Ten Day directly. Teacher Yang asked the class to stand silent and remember what day it was. Teacher Yu told them that today they must think about the sufferings of the Chinese people.

On their way home from school, Shao-shao and Yun-lung stopped to buy mulberry leaves for their silkworms.

"How many cocoons have you got?" Yun-lung asked.

"Ten this morning."

"Any yellow?"

"None yet. How about you?"

"One so far. Come see it when we get home."

"Really?" Yellow cocoons were rare and highly prized. "I'll check mine first. Maybe I've got a yellow cocoon by now."

When Shao-shao passed the family room on his way upstairs, he heard Second Brother giving Fourth Sister advice about the Middle School teachers. "When Old Wong asks a question, raise your hand and tell him all you know right away. Then he won't bother you again. He goes after people who are silent."

Last year, when Fourth Sister was in sixth grade, she used to give Shao-shao advice. Now that she was in Middle School, she had new friends and new teachers, and she spent hardly any time with him.

He knelt by the cardboard box at the foot of the bed, counting cocoons. While he'd been at school, three fat, white caterpillars had wrapped themselves in silk thread. Shao-shao spread a few mulberry leaves on his palm and picked up a silkworm. He liked to watch them eat. They were always hungry, and he was sure they were happy when he brought them food, as happy as a dumb insect could be.

In one corner of the box, another silkworm had started its cocoon. Shao-shao could see it through the thin cradle of silk, moving its head up and down, spitting out thread.

He put the silkworm back in the box, jumped up, ran downstairs and out the door to find Yun-lung.

Late sunlight slanted over the courtyard. Shao-shao's friends were playing marbles, while the little Shih boys next door banged sticks against their house, screaming with glee. Across from them, Li-sha sat on her front steps, watching the other children. When she met his eyes, he turned away, as if he had not seen her, and knocked on Yun-lung's door.

"I've got a yellow one, too. The silkworm's making it now!" he told Yun-lung.

"I'm still ahead of you. I've got another one. Come see."

After Shao-shao had admired his friend's silkworms, Yun-lung said, "Let's go play marbles."

"I don't know. We've got so much math homework. Father saw my last test, with all the red marks on it, and he was mad." Father usually did not know when Shao-shao had a test, but he had found this one next to his chair. Shao-shao had not left it there. He suspected Second Brother, but he had no proof.

"Just one game won't hurt," Yun-lung said as they

went downstairs. "It'll be fun with so many people."

Pei-fu and Tai-shen, two of their classmates, had stopped on their way home for a game with Tak-ming, Yun-lung's older brother.

"Come on, Shao-shao," Tak-ming called when he saw them. "We need a lefty in this game."

One game wouldn't take much time. Shao-shao picked a marble from his pocket, squatted, rolled it on his palms, blew warm breath on his shooting fingers, and aimed carefully. He was the only one in the neighborhood who played marbles left-handed.

His blue marble ambled toward the first couple of holes as if it knew just where it was going. Out of the corner of his eye, he saw Li-sha come closer to watch the game.

His marble reached the next hole, and the next.

"Getting too close," Tak-ming cried when Shao-shao's marble reached the fourth hole while his lay stranded near the sixth.

Pei-fu, his thick hair rumpled in the wind, leaned back on his heels, puffing out his cheeks, waiting his turn. He'd gotten another slap on the hand this morning for his clumsy calligraphy. Tai-shen traced patterns in the dust with a grimy finger.

"Lefty's gonna miss, gonna miss, gonna miss," chanted Pei-fu.

But Shao-shao didn't miss. His blue marble sped toward the hole as if it belonged there. He let out the breath he'd been holding. His face relaxed into a grin. One more shot and he'd be ahead of Tak-ming!

Tak-ming groaned; Yun-lung cheered; Pei-fu

31

hooted; Tai-shen whistled. Shao-shao looked up quickly to see Li-sha smile. Across the courtyard, the Shih boys made noises like machine guns, paying no attention to the game.

Mother put her head out the family room window.

"You'd better come in now," she called down to Shao-shao. "Your father will be home any minute."

Shao-shao hardly heard her. He bounced on his heels, his marbles swinging in his pockets. "Watch out, Tak-ming. Here I come."

"Quiet, everybody. Let the sharpshooter concentrate," said Yun-lung, as Shao-shao crouched down once more, shifting balance on his sneakers. And they were quiet, even Pei-fu, not even breathing, as Shao-shao took aim.

"Shao-shao!" This was not Mother's voice but Father's, harsh with anger, rumbling like faraway antiaircraft guns. Shao-shao dropped his marble, stood, and turned. His father's face was flushed. Under the brim of his hat, a vein in his temple throbbed.

Father raised his arm, pointing up at their house.

"Why aren't you in there studying? Why do I always find you playing marbles in the dirt? Soiling your clothes, wasting your time, disgracing us with your marks—what a useless boy you are! When I was your age, I had to work after school in my father's shop. All you ever do is play!"

Li-sha ducked into her house. The boys froze, watching Father drop his hand, dismiss Shao-shao with a gesture of disgust, and stride through his front door.

For a moment, no one said anything.

Then Pei-fu chanted, "Bad boy, bad boy," shaking his finger at Shao-shao. Tak-ming and Tai-shen took up the chant, and the Shih boys gleefully joined in. "Little boy got a scolding, Little boy got a scolding."

Shame burned the moment, clear and sharp as a movie in slow motion, into Shao-shao's memory.

Yun-lung punched Shao-shao gently on the arm and whispered, "See you tomorrow."

Shao-shao plodded toward his house, his fists clenched, bending his head so they could not see how his cheeks burned. He had been so close to winning, and Father had to spoil it all. Again.

Shao-shao stood in the vestibule, closed doors on either side of him. The downstairs parlor and dining room were kept shut most of the time, for the family hardly ever used them.

He could hear Father's slippered feet cross the family room, hear Father greet the rest of the family, hear Fourth Sister tell Father how many math problems she had finished. Father wouldn't care how she did them, if she understood the math or not, Shao-shao thought bitterly. He just wanted to see his children studying.

Shao-shao looked at his slippers, sitting at the foot of the stairs, but he did not put them on. Instead he turned and trudged out the door into the darkening courtyard.

Everyone had gone home.

Head down, eyes on his scuffed sneakers, Shao-shao wandered across the courtyard, out the gate, and down the alley past the high wall around Li-sha's garden. He bit his lip, determined not to cry, even though no one could see him. Li-sha's jump rope twanged through the air, her feet bounced against hard earth, her soft voice counted.

Then the rhythm stopped, and she called out to him.

It was getting dark. No one would know. He touched the delicate stems of the cast-iron lotus flowers on her garden gate. Long ago, the Frenchman who built the house had installed a fancy openwork iron gate. No one else in the neighborhood had anything like it. Tonight, someone must have left it unlatched, because it swung open easily, admitting Shao-shao to the small garden behind Li-sha's house.

"One of my birds got out today," she said. "Mother was feeding them, and it slipped through the door before she could catch it. It flew all over the living room and made my little brother laugh."

"Did you get it back?"

"Yes. I lured it with seed. I think it was tired anyway."

"Do your birds sing?"

"No. But they sure chatter a lot."

"Doesn't your father mind?"

"Papa? No, he bought them for me."

The ache in Shao-shao's throat eased a bit. Tears no longer pressed against his eyes.

"Don't you ever take them out to air?"

"I took them in the garden last summer, but it's too cold now. Do you want to see them?"

Shao-shao didn't know what to answer. He did want to see them, but if he told her so she might invite him in. Before he could speak, Li-sha's back door opened and her father came out.

"Shao-shao," he said, with a friendly smile. "I'm happy to see you. But it's time for Li-sha to come in. Her supper's ready." He looked slender and relaxed in his Western shirt, open at the collar.

Shao-shao silently looked at his shoes, not daring to meet Mr. Chen's eyes.

Mr. Chen took Li-sha's hand. He seemed too young to be anyone's father. "Come again," he told Shao-shao, "you're welcome anytime."

Shao-shao mumbled his thanks, embarrassed, and turned back toward his house. It was nearly dinner-time. If he didn't go home soon, Mother would send Second Brother to look for him. From the courtyard he saw Mother's outline behind the blinds of the second-floor window.

When he entered the vestibule, she was making her slow way down the stairs, leaning on the rail.

"Shao-shao." She spoke softly, intensely. "Where have you been all this time? Why didn't you wear your hat? It's getting cold."

Shao-shao hung up his coat, pulled off his shoes, and put on his slippers. "Why did he have to tell me off in front of my friends?" he grumbled, staring at the worn carpet.

Mother put her arm around his shoulders and opened the door of the dim, stale-smelling downstairs parlor.

"He doesn't want you to waste the advantages he's given you."

"What advantages? All he wants me to do is work. He never wants me to have any fun."

Mother drew Shao-shao over to sit on the slippery silk cushion of the rosewood couch. "He never had much fun when he was your age, you know. He grew up in the poorest section of Chung-ming. You've only seen Hong Kong and Shanghai. You don't know how poor the rest of China is."

Shao-shao clasped his hands together, trying to hang on to his anger. His parents always told him what hard childhoods they'd had. As if that should make him grateful.

"Every day he came straight home from school to work in his father's store. He never had time to play marbles. By the time he was your age, Grandfather took a new wife. She was very mean to him and his older brother."

Shao-shao hunched his shoulders and shivered. Mr. Wu next door had two wives. Shao-shao didn't like to think of a stranger coming into their house, even a young and pretty one. Yet he couldn't imagine Father as a weak and helpless child.

"Then his mother died, and his life was so unbearable that he and his brother ran away. Shao-shao, they had no home. They had to beg for food, until a kind man adopted them. Then they worked in his bakery shop. Father never went to school again. Everything else he learned, he taught himself. So you see how lucky you are, compared to him. Even during the war, we can afford to send you to school."

Shao-shao didn't feel lucky, but he knew better than to say so. Anyway, he'd heard part of this story before. But no one had ever told him what happened to Father's older brother, his first uncle. Now, he didn't care to ask.

Upstairs, they could hear Gao-ma and Ah-fong arranging the chairs around the family-room table. From the kitchen came the warm, spicy smells of supper. Shao-shao stood up, still hanging his head.

"Time for supper." Mother gave him a gentle push up the stairs.

Walking up, he remembered Double Ten Day, the Birthday of the Chinese Republic. It was almost over, and no one had been able to celebrate.

4. Cocoons Burst

October 1944

"HE NEVER LETS ME HAVE ANY FUN," Shao-shao grumbled as Gao-ma walked him home from school.

"He wants what is best for you," Gao-ma replied as she always did. "He wants you to study hard so you can go abroad and make lots of money."

"He never takes me to the movies, he won't let me have a goldfish or a bird, he scolds me when I read kung-fu novels. I can't study all the time!"

"Children should obey their parents," Gao-ma said firmly.

It was no use talking to her. She was no more sympathetic than Third Sister, who had told him: "Don't blame Father. He's got more on his mind than you know."

Shao-shao knew she meant Father's work for the underground. Besides selling cotton cloth before the war, Father had worked for Chiang Kai-shek's Na-

38

tionalist government. Half-heard fragments of conversations, oblique remarks from his parents and older sisters made Shao-shao believe that Father still helped the Nationalists. But in secret. And he did more than smuggle cloth.

Shao-shao looked down the long, narrow street. He saw no one but a child and a grown-up far ahead. He could run to their alley and not leave Gao-ma's sight.

He spread out his arms and roared from deep in his chest, an American bomber whizzing over the Bund. Soon he had caught up with Li-sha and her servant.

"Hi, Shao-shao," she said, as if they were old friends. "Where's Yun-lung?"

"He's sick. He threw up all last night."

She made a sympathetic noise, then asked, "How'd you do on the math test?"

"Messed up one or two problems. I don't know about the rest. Okay, I think. How about you?"

"I'm not very good at math. My father helps me with my homework, but I don't always understand him, so I don't do well on tests. I'll be glad if I get a C."

They reached the corner of the alley. Shao-shao looked back to see Gao-ma frowning as she hurried to catch up. Soon they must pass through the courtyard gateway. If he went with Li-sha, everyone would see them together.

He passed Li-sha and entered the courtyard alone. Inside the gate, he almost collided with Li-sha's father, but he swerved just in time, and came to rest on his own front steps, where he sat panting and waiting for Gao-ma.

If Mr. Chen knew how close Shao-shao had come, he gave no sign. He was saying good-bye to three visitors, small men dressed in Western suits, but he did not smile and look the men in the face as Father would. Instead he bowed as Japanese do, and the men bowed back. They spoke in Japanese.

Shao-shao went tense all over. He felt a prickle along his spine, and knew how a cat felt when it hissed.

"Ah, Li-sha." Mr. Chen beamed as his daughter entered the courtyard. He put his hand on her shoulder and told the men proudly, "This is my first daughter."

Smiles and bobbing heads. "Very pretty," one said. "I have a daughter your age back home," said another. Although they spoke Chinese, Shao-shao could hardly understand them. Li-sha returned their smiles.

Turning to leave, the Japanese men met Gao-ma coming through the gateway. She kept her head down and her shoulders drawn in as she passed them. She did not look up until she pushed Shao-shao into the house and closed the door behind them.

"Japs!" She stomped into the kitchen. Shao-shao followed her and watched as she dropped a pinch of tea leaves into her cup. Her hand trembled so that half the leaves scattered on the table. She used both hands to lift the heavy iron kettle that always boiled on the great black stove. Even so, she spilled water. Shao-shao ran for a cloth to wipe it up.

She fell into a chair and braced her elbows on the kitchen table, trying to keep her hands from shaking. "Traitor pig! With *his* education he should be with our government in Chungking, not here bowing to the Japs!" She spat out each word. "Some day he'll pay for what he's done!"

Cocoons filled Shao-shao's cardboard box. They were pressed into all the corners. He counted them every day. Twenty-six, three of them yellow.

The weather had turned colder, and dark came so early no one thought of playing marbles after school. Shao-shao's cricket stopped singing and would hardly move, even when Shao-shao tickled it. Every night, Shao-shao came straight home from school, checked his cocoons, and started his homework. When Father arrived, he smiled to see his children sitting around the table. Shao-shao would watch him reading the newspaper, wishing he would look up and smile proudly at Shao-shao, the way Li-sha's father did when he introduced her to his Japanese friends.

One afternoon Shao-shao bent over to survey the cardboard box, then dropped to his knees beside it. There was a hole in one of the cocoons.

Shao-shao examined each cocoon in turn. One other had opened. He looked around his room. Two white moths clung to the wall over his bed.

Another moth struggled out of its cocoon. Gently, Shao-shao touched its still-moist, furry head, remembering a hungry silkworm crawling across his palm, voraciously devouring mulberry leaves.

That silkworm had become a moth. A moth that would lay eggs that would hatch into silkworms that would turn into moths. Around and around, like a prayer wheel. Shao-shao ran down to the family room and grabbed a sheet of newspaper from a stack on the carved daybed. Fourth Sister, at the dining table, looked up from her homework.

"Cocoons are bursting," he said.

She followed him up the stairs and watched as he slipped the newspaper under the two moths on the wall, forcing them to lift their damp, furred feet and step onto it. Slowly, he lowered the moths, on the sheet of newspaper, to his bed. Now they would lay their eggs on the paper, not on the wall. If he could collect enough eggs, he might be able to keep them alive and hatch his own silkworms.

As the last light from the window faded, another moth broke out of its cocoon and fluttered away.

Fourth Sister pried an empty cocoon from the cardboard box and plucked the frayed strands of silk. "It's no good now," she said. "The thread's all cut up." She pointed to the other cocoons. "We should drop some in boiling water and unwind the thread."

"No you won't!" What a horrible thought: his well-fed, trusting silkworms, happily asleep in their cocoons, boiled alive, as if they'd been raised in a silk factory. "Anyway, what would you do with such a tiny bit of thread?" he asked Fourth Sister.

42

"I could weave a shroud for your cricket." Fourth Sister looked at the cricket pot and laughed, crushing the empty cocoon between her fingertips.

That night at dinner, Father greeted Shao-shao with a mocking smile. "Did your homework upstairs, I see," he said, looking as if he knew Shao-shao had not opened a book. He had taken off his jacket, but had not yet changed into the Chinese gown he wore at home. The shirt, tie, and vest made him look forbidding.

"Just a few more problems to finish," Shao-shao mumbled into the rice bowl he held close to his mouth. "Teacher Liu gave us a lot of homework."

"Good for Teacher Liu," Father replied, looking so wise and satisfied that Shao-shao knew he was safe. Father would pay no more attention to him. He would never look at Shao-shao's assignment, so he would never know Shao-shao had not started yet.

After dinner, Shao-shao went straight upstairs to work out math problems. The moths fluttered around the room, circling his desk lamp, landing on his papers and beating their wings.

"*Ai-ya!* What a mess!" said Gao-ma when she came to put him to bed.

"Let me finish," Shao-shao pleaded. "I've only got a couple more problems."

Gao-ma sputtered her annoyance as she surveyed the fluttering moths, the newspaper beaded with eggs, the empty cocoons.

43

"Don't hurt the eggs," Shao-shao cried, as she lifted up the sheet of newspaper. "I want to hatch them."

"Hatch?" Gao-ma shook her head, but slid her open hand carefully under the newspaper so it would not crumple. "I'll put it under your bed so the eggs won't get stepped on."

She turned down his bed and laid out his pajamas, then called Fourth Sister. As he put on his pajamas, he heard Fourth Sister come up, heard Gao-ma coax and scold her out of her clothes and into her nightgown. Shao-shao got in bed and pulled the comforter, heavy with cotton padding, over his cheek. He did not feel sleepy.

When Gao-ma came to turn off his light, he sat straight up and said, "Tell me a story!"

Gao-ma could read no more than a dozen characters. She had left her village as a young widow to work as a servant in the city and earned enough money to buy land near her village, but she never returned. Yet she remembered every word of the tales she had heard from her mother and from traveling storytellers.

Fourth Sister stood in the doorway to Shao-shao's room. "Please, Gao-ma. You haven't told a story since we started school."

Gao-ma looked at Fourth Sister and back at Shao-shao. Her soft cheeks crinkled into a smile, her gold tooth gleamed in the lamplight. "So you haven't gotten too old for stories?" She sank down on the foot of Shao-shao's bed and reached out her arm to gather Fourth Sister next to her.

"There's only one story I should tell tonight," she said, looking at a moth on the windowsill. "About the Cowherd and the Weaving Maid."

"Oh yes," said Fourth Sister, leaning her head on Gao-ma's shoulder. "I like that one."

So Gao-ma began. "Once long ago, in a far-off village in Kweilin Province, an orphan boy lived with his elder brother's family. The brother treated the boy like a stepson. He gave him the worst of everything and made him sleep in the cow shed with the water buffalo."

Shao-shao wrapped his arms tightly around his knees. He imagined the younger brother, lonely for his parents, going out to the cow shed to sleep in the hay.

"The younger brother was good-natured, so he did not quarrel. He had always taken care of the water buffalo and he loved it dearly. He talked to it and it seemed to understand, even though it could not reply. He led it as it pulled the plow across the rice fields, and when the plowing was done, he took it to a deep pool fed by a stream running from the faraway mountains. There it fed on thick grass and wallowed happily. Everyone forgot the boy's name and called him 'Cowherd.'"

With open eyes, Shao-shao saw Gao-ma's wrinkled face, her graying hair in its untidy bun. Fourth Sister leaned against her shoulder, staring into space. In his

45

mind's eye he saw a clear stream flowing through green fields. He had always lived in cities, but he had heard about the country from Gao-ma. He could almost smell the new rice shoots, hear clean water tumbling over stones, feel the warm sun on his face as he leaned against the water buffalo's broad back.

"The years passed and the boy grew up. One day his brother, pretending to be kind, told him, 'Now is the time for you to have a home of your own. We'll divide up the property Father left us. You take the buffalo and the cart, and I'll be content with what's left.' "

The imaginary rice field disappeared. A vivid, unwelcome memory took its place, a memory of Shao-shao's first spring in Shanghai, when First Brother took him out to fly a kite. Two of First Brother's friends met them in the field. First Brother had spoken kindly, offering to launch the kite and give it back to Shao-shao. But he passed it to his friends and teased Shao-shao when he asked for the kite, keeping him from taking it. Shao-shao tried to push the memory out of his mind. He did not like to remember himself crying.

"The Cowherd left his village that day. He was not sad, for he had his best friend, the water buffalo, to keep him company. They traveled far into the mountains. The Cowherd settled near the edge of a forest and made his living as a woodcutter."

Shao-shao wondered what it would be like to live alone, with no family, no friends, no city spreading around him. Shao-shao thought he would like doing as he pleased, with no one to tease or scold him, and a kind water buffalo for company.

"One night he heard a voice from the doorway call, 'Cowherd.' No one had spoken to him since he left his village. Who could be calling him?

"The Cowherd looked out of the door and saw the water buffalo. It opened its mouth and called his name again. He was not surprised, for he had always suspected it could talk.

" 'You have been so kind to me,' the water buffalo said, 'that I will tell you a secret. Tomorrow, do not cut wood in the forest. Follow the stream into the mountains until you reach the great pool below the waterfall. There you will see seven beautiful maidens swimming, maidens from the Heavenly Kingdom. Their clothes will be spread on the rocks beside the pool. One gown will be red, the others white. The red gown belongs to the Weaving Maid, the loveliest and wisest of them all. She spins silk thread and weaves cloth for the gods—the finest cloth you can imagine. If you want to marry one of the maidens, you must steal her gown. Then she cannot fly back to the Heavenly Kingdom with the others.' "

Shao-shao felt a cold draft from the window on his back and neck. He slid down, put his head on the pillow, and drew up the comforter, wishing he had a friend like the water buffalo, a friend he could care for, a friend who would tell secrets to him alone.

"The next day, the Cowherd followed his friend's instructions and found the maidens swimming in the pool. No sooner did the young man see the Weaving

Maid than he fell in love. He gathered up the red robe and went to hide in the bushes.

"When the maidens finished their swim, the six shook out their white robes and six white cranes appeared. The cranes carried the maidens into the sky, leaving the Weaving Maid behind. The boy quickly came out of hiding and begged the Weaving Maid to be his wife. Since he spoke so kindly and sincerely and was so good-looking, she consented."

"Why would she leave her palace in Heaven to marry a cowherd?" Fourth Sister turned her head to look up at Gao-ma. "I'd never do that!"

"She was tired of taking orders from the Empress of Heaven," Gao-ma replied. "And she had found her true love. For three years they lived as happily as a pair of wood ducks. The Weaving Maid set to work and soon made enough cloth to buy more land and build a solid house. The Cowherd and the water buffalo worked the land, so they always had enough rice. In time, two children blessed their household.

"They had only one sorrow. The faithful water buffalo reached the end of its days. It whispered to the Cowherd, 'After I die, skin me and save my hide. If you are in trouble, wrap yourself in my skin and it will help you.' "

Warm inside his comforter, lulled by Gao-ma's low, rhythmic voice, Shao-shao thought, the Cowherd deserved a reward for taking such good care of his friend.

"Up in Heaven, the Empress was angry at the Weaving Maid for going to live on earth. Besides, no one in the Heavenly Kingdom could weave such lustrous silk. So the Empress sent guards to search for her. When they found the Weaving Maid, the Empress herself went down to fetch her back to Heaven.

"The Weaving Maid tried to fight off the old woman and cried to her son to fetch his father. But when they returned to the house they found her gone. The Cowherd wept as if his heart would break. Had it not been for his children, he might have taken his own life.

"In the midst of his grief, he remembered the water buffalo's last words. He put his children into two baskets hanging from a pole over his shoulders, wrapped himself in the skin, and stepped outside. Immediately, he found himself flying through the air.

"He broke through the clouds and saw his wife high above him, held tight by an old woman. The water buffalo's hide carried him faster and faster, until he had almost reached them. The Weaving Maid called to her husband, begging him to rescue her.

"When the Empress of Heaven saw the Cowherd gaining on her, she plucked a jade hairpin from her hair and drew a line across the sky, dividing the heavens in two. No sooner had she drawn it than the line became a deep river of stars, the Milky Way. The lovers could see each other across the river, but they could not cross it.

" 'Since the Cowherd keeps the Weaving Maid from her work, he shall live on one side of the river, and she on the other,' the Empress commanded. Instantly, the lovers became two twinkling stars, Altair and Vega, immortal yet forever apart, forever grieving for each other."

Shao-shao hovered near the edge of sleep. With the clarity of a dream, he imagined the Empress's arm outstretched, like Father's when he'd told Shao-shao off for playing marbles.

Gao-ma said: "Their weeping reached the ears of the Emperor of Heaven, who decided to help them. 'Let them meet once a year on the Seventh Day of the Seventh Month,' he decreed.

"The Empress of Heaven reluctantly consented, but she would not make a bridge across the river she had created, so the lovers had no way to meet. The magpies of the earth took pity on them. On the day appointed, they flew up to heaven. Each bird grasped the tail of another in its long beak to make a bridge for the Cowherd.

"And so they meet, every year, those two bright stars on either side of the Milky Way. The Weaving Maid is also the goddess who blesses women's weaving and embroidery. And the poets say it is better to meet only once a year yet be immortal than to live a life together and be parted forever by death."

Far away, through his quilt cocoon, Shao-shao heard Fourth Sister's contented sigh, felt the bed move as she and Gao-ma stood up. Gao-ma leaned over him. He opened his eyes and saw her lift a white moth from the windowsill to her finger. Carefully, she set it with the others on the sheet of paper beneath his bed.

"Sleep well, Shao-shao," she said softly.

50

The distant pop of antiaircraft guns kept Shao-shao from sinking into sleep. American bombers were flying tonight, but not across Shanghai. Gao-ma stood on the landing, listening to the sound.

"Too far north," she muttered softly to herself. Shao-shao knew she was thinking of the son she had left in her village up the Yangtze River.

Her son was not quite right in his mind, but he could work the land she had bought. Though she rarely spoke of him, Shao-shao knew she sent him money every month. Shao-shao turned toward the wall, pulled the comforter over his ears, closed his eyes, and imagined a river of stars flowing forever across a black sky.

5. Long Life
November 1944

"SLOW DOWN, SHAO-SHAO." YUN-LUNG panted.

But Shao-shao couldn't slow down. The streets ahead seemed endless. He wanted to be home. Now.

A chill wind pushed him along. It blew down his collar and pinched his cheeks the way his father's friends did.

"Meet you later!" he called over his shoulder.

Shao-shao ran through the courtyard gate, where the wind could not follow, past Li-sha and her baby brother, past the Shih boys, and into his house, dropping his schoolbag outside the closed doors of the downstairs dining room. Fat Ming had come late last night. What food did he bring? Shao-shao ran into the kitchen to find out.

Gao-ma stood at the kitchen table, using her largest cleaver to slice pork.

The cleaver stopped in midair and she smiled a wide welcome. "The birthday boy has come home."

Ah-fong smiled shyly over her shoulder as she rinsed scallions in a wooden bowl. Food covered the kitchen table: sliced vegetables stacked neatly on plates, one chicken plucked and cut into chunks, a small stack of Mother's special minced-beef balls heaped on a platter, noodles ready to drop in the kettle of broth simmering on the great black stove. They would not use extra rice tonight, even though guests were coming. Tonight the family would eat noodles in honor of Shao-shao's tenth birthday. Long noodles to wish him long life.

The fire burning in the heart of the stove warmed the whole kitchen. Three cats—one black, one orange, and one tabby—sat under Gao-ma's feet, their yellow eyes intent on her movements. His birthday dinner would be ready to cook when the guests arrived. Tonight his family would honor him. No one would scold him or tease him. He would be the center of attention.

The thought made him squirm inside, and remember how he felt when Teacher Yang had struck his palm and made him stand in front of the class. At the same time he was so excited he could hardly stand still.

Gao-ma dumped the strips of pork into a bowl and poured soy sauce and wine over them. She washed her hands and untied her apron strings. She eyed the table. "Not enough," she sighed. "It's a good thing we have plenty of noodles."

She hung up her apron. "When Second Brother had his birthday in Hong Kong, we had two chickens, two kinds of duck, fish, and plenty of beef. You could get anything then."

Shao-shao didn't want to hear about how good things were in Hong Kong. "I'm going to play with Yun-lung," he said quickly.

Gao-ma followed him out of the kitchen, her apron over her arm, shouting, "Don't stay long. Don't get dirty. Remember, it's your birthday."

Yun-lung had not waited in the courtyard, and the Shih boys had gone inside. No one was there, no one but Li-sha and the oldest of her two brothers, tangled up in her jump rope.

"You can't skip with me, Didi," she scolded, "you're too little." When she had untwined the jump rope from his fat, red-trousered leg, she stood up, smiled at Shao-shao, took the little boy's hand, and led him across the space between them.

"Didi, say 'Happy Birthday' to Shao-shao," she said in her sweetest voice.

Li-sha's little brother looked at Shao-shao soberly. He put a finger in his mouth, but said nothing.

Shao-shao looked toward Yun-lung's windows. He couldn't see anyone looking out.

"Who's coming to your party?" she asked.

"First Sister and her husband, Grandmother and Uncle, my cousin. My brothers and sisters, of course."

The boy wriggled and Li-sha let him go. He scampered toward his ball, which had come to rest near Shao-shao's steps.

"I saw your grandmother when she was here

54

before. You're lucky. I hardly remember what my grandparents look like."

"Are they dead?" Shao-shao's grandfather had died long before he was born. But Li-sha's parents were much younger than his. Her grandparents should be alive.

"No, they're up north, in Harbin."

"That's far." So far, it hardly seemed part of China. The Japanese had occupied Harbin Province long before they marched south. "When did you see them last?"

"When we lived with them, while Papa was going to school in Japan. They gave me an American doll for my birthday."

Li-sha's brother trotted back to her. His ball and mitten were covered with dirt. When he plucked at her trousers, soiling them, she grabbed his wrist and pulled his hand away. He started to cry.

"He doesn't remember Father's parents at all," she said, paying no attention to his fussing. "He was only a baby when we left. He'd be happier if there were more people to pay attention to him."

"Shao-shao!" Father's deep voice sounded from the courtyard gate.

Li-sha gathered up the baby, whispered "Happy Birthday," and hurried home.

Father touched Shao-shao's shoulder. "Why aren't you inside washing up?" he asked. "Could it be, *could it be,* you've forgotten what day it is?"

"No!" Shao-shao yelled.

Gao-ma met them at the door, smiling to hear

Father's chuckle. She pushed Shao-shao up the stairs.

Coming close behind them, Father said, "I thought I told you not to play with the Chen girl. If people saw you talking with those collaborators, our family would be shamed."

Shao-shao gave the best excuse he could think of. "I was asking her about homework."

"Ask someone else next time," Father said, but he did not sound angry.

Gao-ma escorted Shao-shao up to his bedroom. She took off his stiff school jacket and hung it up, told him to wash thoroughly, then helped him put on a clean shirt and new silk jacket. He hardly heard her directions or the commotion downstairs as his brother and sisters came home.

Why did Father look so worried? Was he afraid Mr. Chen would find out his connection with Fat Ming?

Gao-ma held out his stiff leather shoes. His feet had grown since Mother bought them, and they were too tight.

"I want my sneakers," he said.

She sighed as she tied the laces of his comfortable cloth shoes. "The others look better," she said. "Like the ones English boys wore."

When Shao-shao entered the family room, Father put down his paper and smiled. He had changed into a long Chinese gown of dark blue silk. He looked relaxed, approachable. He seemed to have forgotten about Li-sha. His mood warmed Shao-shao like soup on a cold night. Tonight Father's smile would last. Tonight he would be kind.

"Happy Birthday," Father said, reaching into his pocket. He held out a small red envelope.

Shao-shao thanked him and took the envelope. Would he ever be as handsome as Father? Mother hugged him and wished him "Happy Birthday" for the second time that day. "Now that you are ten," she told him, "you must study very hard. You have to be at the top of your class to go abroad."

She had told him this so often he knew what she was saying, although he could not hear her over the shouts of his brothers and sisters.

"Happy Birthday!" Third Sister held out a package wrapped in red paper.

Shao-shao tore away string and paper. Inside he found a book of riddles. Third Sister always remembered what he liked. He opened the book and read, "Two people are walking down the street. One is the other's father, but the other isn't his son." He looked at Second Brother. "Who is walking down the street?"

Second Brother stood silent, puzzled.

"What's the answer?" Fourth Sister asked.

"Guess." Third Sister smiled.

"I give up," said Second Brother.

"Me, too." Fourth Sister reached for the book.

Shao-shao pulled it away and looked up at Father, who was smiling and shaking his head. "I can't guess either," he said. "Tell us."

"Father and daughter!" Shao-shao cried triumphantly.

Everyone groaned and laughed because they had been tricked so easily.

Mother interrupted the clamor. "Quick, quick! The guests will be here any minute." Following her orders, the older children put away newspapers and schoolbooks scattered around. Shao-shao stretched to put the riddle book on top of the tall carved chest, where it would be safe. Gao-ma and Ah-fong pulled the round table open and put in extra leaves. It was so big they had to push the sofa back against the wall to make room for it. Ah-fong laid out teacups, plates, and chopsticks. Muttering to herself, Gao-ma counted, while Mother watched to make sure there were chopsticks for everyone.

Through the window, Shao-shao saw First Sister and her husband. They walked across the courtyard with their heads together as if they shared a private joke. They always looked stylish. First Sister had her hair curled at the beauty shop. She had put on a new silk dress for his party. Brother Ma wore his gray suit and set his hat, a gray fedora, at a jaunty angle.

Laughter traveled ahead of them up the stairs and burst in as they cried "Happy Birthday, Shao-shao!" Brother Ma handed Shao-shao a red envelope. First Sister gave him a small narrow box of bright gold, tied with a red ribbon.

He took it, staring up at her, half-guessing, not daring to believe what he guessed.

58

"Go ahead, open it. You're old enough to have one now."

He slipped off the ribbon and opened the box. Resting in its bed of white silk was a green-marbled fountain pen. His brothers and sisters gathered around as he unscrewed the cap and examined the immaculate gold nib.

"Thank your sister, Shao-shao," he heard Mother say, as he stared at the pen.

First Sister smiled expectantly.

"Thank you, thank you, First Sister!" In his excitement Shao-shao spoke louder than he meant to, making everyone laugh.

"Now you have no excuse for poor marks in English," Father said.

But I get good marks in English, even using a pencil, Shao-shao thought. He knew better than to annoy Father by saying it aloud. Besides, he knew his English papers would look better written with a fountain pen. Tomorrow at school, everyone would admire it.

Voices rose up the stairs: Gao-ma welcoming Grandmother into the house. Brother Ma went down at once. Shao-shao put the pen in his pocket and followed Fourth Sister to the second-floor landing, where he could watch Grandmother climb the stairs, helped on one side by Brother Ma and on the other by Second Uncle, Mother's younger brother. Second Uncle always made Shao-shao uncomfortable. He never knew what Uncle might say.

Between the two men, Grandmother looked as small as Li-sha, in her old woman's tunic and trousers of dark brown silk. She paused on the landing by the storage room to catch her breath, as Mother often did. Second Uncle and his daughter, Cousin Wei-fun, had lived with Grandmother since his wife died. Cousin waved at Shao-shao and Fourth Sister from behind her father's shoulder.

Grandmother turned her wrinkled face up toward Shao-shao. "Happy Birthday," she said. Even those familiar words sounded different, because she spoke in the Hangchow dialect. When she reached the top of the stairs, she pulled a red envelope from her purse. Shao-shao knew there would not be much money in it, for Mother and Father helped pay her expenses. But Uncle, too, had an envelope for him. Uncle smiled vacantly.

"Thank you, Grandmother. Thank you, Uncle," Shao-shao said, bowing slightly.

Mother plumped up a sofa cushion and arranged pillows as Uncle and Brother Ma helped Grandmother to her seat. Mother sat down next to Grandmother on the sofa and First Sister pulled up a chair beside her. Cousin Wei-fun and Fourth Sister linked arms and headed for the corner beside the high carved chest, where they could whisper and play with the cats.

"What happened at the track today? The papers never tell these days." Uncle spoke peevishly. No one answered. The racetrack had been closed since the beginning of the Japanese occupation.

Brother Ma nudged Shao-shao's ribs.

"Hey, Shao-shao," he said, "now that you're ten, your teachers won't let you act like a baby. Got your homework done?"

"I did it at school." Brother Ma couldn't catch Shao-shao with his teasing tonight. Shao-shao had given up a precious recess that day so he would not have to do homework at his birthday party.

"Oh, you are a big boy." Brother Ma called up a sarcastic rumble from deep in his large chest. "Let's see it then."

Shao-shao looked around, but his schoolbag was not in the corner with the others. Then he remembered. He'd left it beside the doors to the downstairs dining room. Gao-ma had not been at the door to take it from him, and he had been too excited to think about it.

He ran down to find it lying where he'd left it, grabbed it, and brought it up. When he entered the room again, the babble of conversation ceased as everyone turned to look. Father watched expectantly, half-smiling.

He would show them all what a responsible student he was. Even on his birthday, he had done his mathematics and calligraphy practice.

But the papers were not in his bag. Feeling his face grow hot, he bent his head and rummaged, finding schoolbooks, abacus, ink stick, ink stone, brushes, practice sheets, but no homework.

"Not so big after all?" Brother Ma chuckled.

Shao-shao kept silent. He felt tears stinging behind

his eyes, and he knew they would fall if he spoke.

Brother Ma turned up the cushion of the big upholstered chair to reveal a sheaf of papers. "Could this be what you're looking for, Mister Ten Today?" He held up Shao-shao's homework.

The silence was broken by peals of laughter from all over the room. Brother Ma handed Shao-shao his homework, his big frame shaking with glee at the success of his joke. Father laughed, too.

Shao-shao hung his head, choked with embarrassment. First Sister put her arm around his shoulders.

"Don't be so serious," she whispered. "We're all proud of you."

Eleven bowls of noodles, bigger than rice bowls, ringed the table while Gao-ma and Ah-fong laid out Shao-shao's favorite dishes. The portions might be small, but there was enough for everyone: pork and pickled vegetables, chicken and snow peas, dofu and mushrooms, and the steamed beef balls they called lion's head. Mother cooked lion's head because everyone liked it, but she never ate it herself. A devout Buddhist, she would not eat beef.

Shao-shao spooned lion's head over his noodles, held the bowl close to his mouth, and went to work with his chopsticks. Ah-fong refilled his bowl when he emptied it. He ate two bowls of noodles and meat without stopping, then paused to look around the table. Everyone was talking, eating, or laughing. Every pair of chopsticks moved. Mother delicately laid a choice morsel over Grandmother's noodles.

62

Cousin Wei-fun and Fourth Sister giggled, their heads close together. The cats sat near them on the floor, looking hopefully for a morsel of food the girls were forbidden to give, but often did. Father and Brother Ma spoke of the latest air raids.

". . . right on target, even with the cloud cover." Brother Ma tapped the table with his finger.

"They've got some secret instrument." Father looked as certain as if he had just spoken with the American high command.

They were all here—except First Brother. All celebrating because of him, the youngest one. For his tenth birthday.

Ah-fong refilled the teapots at each end of the table. The meal was nearly finished. Soon, too soon, his birthday would be over. He would have to wait ten long years for another one as important. He could not imagine being twenty.

First Sister caught Shao-shao's eye and smiled as if she read his mind. "Remember the day he was born?" she asked Mother.

Mother smiled fondly at Shao-shao. "Very well," she said. "What a fuss Fourth Sister made when I went off to the hospital."

Fourth Sister put out her lip in a mock pout. "Don't blame me. I was just a baby then."

"I told you not to cry, that you'd get a baby brother," said First Sister. "But that made you cry harder and say you wanted a sister."

Everyone laughed. The separate conversations

stopped as the family joined in remembering.

"We had good times in Hong Kong," Father said. "We had lots of money then."

"No Japs, that was the best." Second Brother handed his empty bowl to Ah-fong.

"And the weather. Always so warm. We could go swimming in Repulse Bay." First Sister sighed and smiled at Brother Ma.

Shao-shao remembered going to the beach with First Sister. They walked on soft sand, swam in warm blue water. First Sister used to meet Brother Ma there. He had always been kind to Shao-shao then. Soon after, Brother Ma and First Sister were married.

"We all thought we'd be safe there." Brother Ma shook his head ruefully.

"Why shouldn't we think so?" Mother leaned forward, vehement, commanding attention. "Hong Kong is part of the British Empire. It was defended by the British Navy. We had almost ten years there without warlords or Japanese bandits. And, don't forget, Shao-shao is a British subject."

Father had always told Shao-shao how lucky he was to be born in Hong Kong, where Father had moved his textile business when the Japanese began their invasion of the northern provinces. Shao-shao was the only member of the Li family entitled by birth to a British passport. Mother always said that when the war was over Shao-shao would go to England and study to be a doctor. To Shao-shao, England seemed as far away as the Heavenly Kingdom in Gao-ma's stories, a place to be visited only in dreams.

Mother had a paper she had gotten from the British hospital in Hong Kong, Shao-shao's birth certificate. Since Shao-shao's brothers and sisters had all been born in China, not one of them had such a paper. Mother kept it in the safest place she could think of, in a box under her mattress with five gold bars. Once she had shown it to Shao-shao.

The square letters of the English alphabet, printed in red, looked ugly to him. They ran in lifeless horizontal rows across stiff paper. Beneath the rows, a pen had been used to write round, regular British script. Shao-shao's name and his parents' names were brushed in proper vertical lines below.

"If he's British, he should be with them!" Second Brother punched Shao-shao on the arm. Shao-shao punched back, but Mother's voice, sharp as a teacher's cane, stopped them both.

"Li Chung, don't you ever say such a thing again!"

All British subjects—men, women, and children, too—now lived in prison camps in the Chapei District, north of the city.

Second Brother imitated a machine gun. "The Japs shelled the British till they gave up!" He could not stay silent for long.

A month after Shao-shao's seventh birthday, the Japanese took over Hong Kong. Father and the other Chinese who had hoped to escape the war in Hong Kong had no place else to go. So most of them went back where they came from. The Japanese didn't care. By then, they occupied most of the Chinese coastland.

Shao-shao remembered the crowded train that took them back to Shanghai.

"At least we don't have to speak Cantonese anymore." Fourth Sister grinned and bobbed her head like a Cantonese opera singer, mimicking the whining, choppy Hong Kong dialect.

They all laughed, even Grandmother. Shao-shao wished he could keep that moment forever. But the laughter fragmented into separate conversations. Before long, the meal was over and it was time to go to bed.

"Let me take your money. We'll use it for clothes," Mother said. He counted the money in the red envelopes before giving it to her. Thirty dollars. The most he had ever gotten.

He rearranged his schoolbag, smoothed his homework, and put it carefully inside. He filled the fountain pen with ink and laid it across the red envelopes on the dresser beside his bed.

Empty red envelopes. All that was left of his birthday.

6. Sunday Expedition
December 1944

EVERYONE ADMIRED THE FOUNTAIN PEN, even Teacher Yang. Shao-shao liked the solid feel of it. Yun-lung tried it, but he scratched the paper and blotted the ink. Li-sha watched from her seat. Shao-shao could tell she wanted to try it, too. Sometime when no one was around, he might let her.

After Shao-shao's birthday, dark came earlier, and the boys went straight home after school. It was too cold to play outside. As they walked home one afternoon, Yun-lung said, "Want to go to the Old City on Sunday?"

Shao-shao went warm with excitement. "I'll ask Gao-ma. She'll let us do more than your servant."

"No servants, just us—and Tai-shen, of course."

"My father would say it's too risky and that I should stay home and study. I'll ask Mother and tell you tomorrow."

Mother made Shao-shao promise never to let his friends out of his sight, not to show his money, to keep his hat and gloves on, to come home before dark, but in the end she said he could go.

When Sunday morning came, Shao-shao double-knotted his sneakers and checked his pockets once more for money. The rhythmic clanging of bells from the French church might be loud enough to cover the sound of his footsteps on the stairs.

Low voices came from the family room. A man sat across from Father resting his fleshy arms on the table. Fat Ming. Shao-shao had never heard his given name. He was overweight, so everyone called him "Fat Ming." He held an envelope in his dumpling hand. Father was listening too carefully to notice Shao-shao.

"... with tomorrow's shipment ..." Curious, Shao-shao stopped for a moment to listen.

"My third daughter can write so small we could hide the whole message in a trouser cuff." Shao-shao heard, and realized Father might look his way any minute. He tiptoed downstairs.

Yun-lung waited in the courtyard, bouncing up and down to keep warm, blowing clouds of breath. "What's keeping Tai-shen?" he asked.

"Maybe his parents changed their minds," Shao-shao said.

Then Tai-shen ran through the courtyard gate. He stood beside them, panting, and pulled off his fur-lined leather hat. "Mother made me wear it," he said as he squeezed it together, wrapped the earflaps around it, and stuffed it into his pocket. "Let's go!" he cried.

They jogged up the alley to Nanking Road, punching each other and laughing. A few well-dressed Chinese hurrying toward the French church smiled vaguely as they passed.

To Shao-shao, the day stretched ahead like a broad avenue, beckoning, limitless. "Let's look for the magician," he yelled.

"Let's eat fried dumplings," Yun-lung yelled back.

"Let's raid the toy store," Tai-shen added, and they all cheered.

The streetcar rumbled down Nanking Road toward the Bund, the waterfront along the Whangpoo River. The car stopped often for passengers, and soon there were no more empty seats. People filled the aisles.

Shao-shao was nearly smothered by a woman in a heavy blue coat who pressed against him as the car made a sharp turn toward its destination. It was not going to the Bund, but to the old Chinese city crowded between the river and the French Sector. Through the dusty window, Shao-shao caught the gleam of bayonets.

The streetcar passed under the gate of the Old City. There Japanese soldiers stood guard. One soldier gave the streetcar a bored glance as it went by. For a moment, Shao-shao looked into his eyes, cold as stones. Then he lurched into the blue-coated woman as the streetcar turned through narrow, winding streets, making sharp turns and unexpected, jerky stops.

Tai-shen reached for the bell pull, giving his

friends an inquiring look. They nodded vigorously. The three boys struggled out of the back door into another world.

They had left the calm boulevards, the spacious courtyards, the comfortable European-style houses of the French Sector far behind. Ramshackle wooden buildings leaned toward each other over winding, erratic streets. Pastel laundry fluttered from bamboo poles thrust out of second-story windows. The scent of roasted chestnuts, fried dumplings, and incense floated on the chill air. Chinese opera—high-pitched chanting punctuated by sudden bursts of percussion—blared from shop radios. Children spilled from sidewalk to street, noisy at their play; parents scolded at the top of their voices. Out of a dark chamber beyond an open door came the click of mah-jongg tiles. Chickens clucked and cackled from their baskets. In a murky alley, silent cats explored garbage cans.

Shao-shao kept his hands in his jacket pockets, holding tight to his money. Any stranger could be a pickpocket. An ancient beggar, wrapped in rags, gnawing on a turnip, sat in the sun outside the Red Lantern bookstore. A small child who might have been the old man's grandson grabbed at passersby, wheedling for pennies. Shao-shao eyed him, sure he would leave them alone. He would know that other children had no money to spare.

They edged their way around the beggar into the dim bookstore where three old men, a pair of girl students, and a boy stood silently reading beside shelves and tables filled with books.

"Ching-tien's Revenge," Tai-shen whispered, picking up a book with an old-style brush painting of two fierce eagles on the cover. "That's a new one."

"No," Shao-shao whispered back. "Second Brother has it. It's about a weak, skinny kid everyone picks on. A Shaolin priest disguised as a beggar teaches him kung fu, and in the end he's stronger than anyone. You'd like it."

Tai-shen tucked the book under his arm while they looked over the others. Shao-shao found a new kung-fu book: *Stranger at Shaolin.* The bookseller wrapped each volume in brown paper and tied it with string. Shao-shao pushed his down into his pants pocket.

"Where now?" asked Tai-shen.

"Candy," said Yun-lung. "Toys," said Shao-shao. They both spoke at once.

"The candy store's on the way to the toy store if we take Bird Street," Tai-shen suggested.

The boys teetered along the curb in single file, for bamboo cages of birds spilled over most of the sidewalk. The birds perched, docile and silent, behind bars. If a bird was lucky, a Buddhist would buy it to release as an act of charity that would be rewarded in the next life. If a bird was unlucky, someone would buy it to cook for dinner. Shao-shao wished some rich Buddhist would buy them all. He did not like to look at them.

As they passed, an old woman in shabby clothes gave the birdman a copper coin. He plucked a bird from the cage and handed it to her. Shao-shao hung back to see what she would do.

She threw it up into the sky. "Fly free," she whispered, and closed her eyes in prayer.

Shao-shao watched the bird fly up into a cold blue sky. He wondered where it would find food, when people starved every day. Perhaps some child would feed it.

Shao-shao didn't want to spend his money. He glanced around the candy store, impatient for his friends to pick out their sweets and leave. Lollipops in a glass jar caught his eye, glowing like jewels in the light from the doorway—red, yellow, green.

Li-sha liked lollipops, he knew. He had seen her sucking one several times.

"Give me an orange lollipop," Shao-shao told the shopkeeper.

"Skinflint broke down after all," Yun-lung teased, stuffing a sizable bag of candy into his coat pocket.

The sudden, brassy sound of a gong made them turn their heads. "Hear that?" Shao-shao asked, pointing his chin down the street. He was glad of the interruption. Anything to deflect Yun-lung's attention. "Acrobats!"

Heads down, hands in their pockets, the boys pushed through the crowd, drawn by the beat of gong and drum and the chanting voice calling, "Come and see, come and see the greatest acrobats in the entire city of Shanghai!"

Once they saw the performers, Shao-shao could not contain his excitement. He poked Yun-lung hard, shouting in his ear, "See the old man? He's the best!"

The acrobats built a pyramid, with the father and sons on the bottom, the girls standing on their shoulders, the youngest on top. As the audience cheered and the mother passed the bowl for coins, they leaped apart lightly, swiftly, breaking up the pyramid. One of the sons sprang onto his father's back, kicked his heels up, and balanced upside down on his father's head.

Shao-shao marveled as the father and his upside-down son made identical gestures. How could this boy stay so effortlessly on his father's head, when Shao-shao couldn't even balance on the floor? One of the sisters handed them each a cup of tea and the crowd laughed and cheered as the father sipped normally, while the boy smiled and drank his cup upside down.

"Why doesn't the tea run down?" Yun-lung asked.

Shao-shao thought: The boy must trust his father completely.

The son leaped down as easily as he had mounted, and the family collected sticks and plates so quickly they seemed to have plucked them out of the air. With a stick topped by a spinning plate in each hand, the acrobats pranced around, then started another pyramid, always keeping the plates spinning on top of their sticks. Were they afraid a plate would drop? They looked so confident, poised on each other's shoulders, smiling proudly, their plates humming.

Yun-lung pulled at Shao-shao's sleeve. "Let's go," he said. "I'm hungry."

"I want to stay and watch the magician."

"Me, too," Tai-shen said.

The bowl passed once more; the family bowed and stepped back, leaving the white-bearded grandfather alone in the circle. He turned and gestured, his long black sleeves swinging, as the woman chanted and struck the gong in a slow, mysterious rhythm. At the sudden beat of her drums, he pulled a string of brightly colored scarves from his sleeve and flourished them in the air.

"That's not hard," Yun-lung whispered.

"Shush!"

The old man dipped ceremoniously into his other sleeve and found there a white pigeon that clung fluttering to his fingers.

How did he do it? Shao-shao could never figure out, no matter how closely he watched.

The magician turned cold water to boiling by pouring it over a brick. For his grand finale, he lighted a torch and swallowed the flames, easy as noodles.

Shao-shao cheered and pulled a penny from his pocket to toss into the bowl.

"Let's eat!" Yun-lung shouted. Shao-shao ran after his friends, following the smell of fried noodles. Suddenly, he felt as if he had not eaten for days.

The toy store in the Old City had more toys than all the shops in the French concession put together. Comfortably full, his fingers warm, Shao-shao stood in the narrow aisle and let his eyes travel leisurely upward over shelves crammed with toys: clay figures from the Peking Opera grouped around a pagoda;

cricket pots; crayons; harmonicas; drums; king-fu comic books to rent or buy; puppets; net bags of marbles; tops; Ping-Pong paddles; balls for Ping-Pong, soccer, and basketball; wooden swords and spears; lanterns. Shao-shao looked up and up to the ceiling where kites hung in dizzying variety. Dragons, centipedes, flowers, butterflies. How could he choose?

"Like my new cricket pot?" Tai-shen asked.

"You still have crickets?" Shao-shao marveled.

"No, they died. This is for next year."

"If you're going to buy something, you'd better do it now." Yun-lung came up beside them, holding a Ping-Pong paddle. "It's getting late."

Shao-shao counted his money. There was enough for a butterfly kite.

Shadows darkened the narrow streets. The three shared a bag of steaming chestnuts, roasted in a brazier over hot coals. Shao-shao tossed his from hand to hand. When it had cooled enough to eat, he bit through burnt skin to chew the soft, white flesh.

Wedged between his friends, trying to protect the butterfly kite from damage, Shao-shao could only laugh when the streetcar's sudden stops threw him off balance. He couldn't fall. The car was too crowded. He and his friends laughed so hard they missed their stop and had to get off at the next one. They did not return along Nanking Road, with its crowds and beggars, but took back streets home.

After Nanking Road and the Chinese city, the

French Sector seemed emptier than ever. On a back street they met four boys bouncing a soccer ball on the sidewalk. The tallest, a classmate of Second Brother's, called Shao-shao by name. He challenged them to a coin-tossing contest.

Shao-shao looked at Yun-lung and Tai-shen. They were as scared of these big boys as he was. Yet they all had spent hours tossing coins for fun. Here was a chance to win a copper or two.

Tai-shen, the oldest, negotiated the rules. When they had all agreed, one of the older boys carefully leaned four copper coins along the wall next to the sidewalk.

Shao-shao felt in his pocket. He had just four coppers left. He pulled out one, warmed it and his cold hands with his breath, and went down on one knee, balancing himself by extending his other leg. He focused on the target, holding the coin between thumb and finger. Then he tossed it. His aim was true; he struck the other coin and knocked it down. Smiling, he scooped up both coins.

Tai-shen and Yun-lung did well, too. They soon took all four coins. Then it was Tai-shen's turn to set the coins up and give the older boys a chance. They were such clumsy shots they lost two coins. When the younger boys won again, the tall one shouted angrily at Yun-lung, "You cheated. I saw you step over the line."

"I did not." Yun-lung stamped his foot and clenched his fists. "You're a sore loser."

76

The squat, moon-faced boy moved closer to Yun-lung. "I saw you step over the line, too. Give back that copper."

"I will not!" Yun-lung thrust his fists deep in his pockets. "I did not step over the line!"

The older boy grabbed his arms, growling, "I'll take it back, you runty cheater." Shao-shao and Tai-shen jumped forward to defend their friend, but the others were stronger and bigger.

A fist slammed Shao-shao full in the face. Lights danced before his eyes and a warm, salty fluid seemed to fill his nose and mouth. Staggering back, he wiped his nose and saw blood on the back of his hand. It was all he could do to keep from sobbing. His friends weren't doing any better: Yun-lung's jacket was ripped, and Tai-shen was helpless after being punched in the stomach.

The bigger boys grabbed their parcels from the toy store and ran off, shouting, "Serves you right, cheaters."

There was nothing Shao-shao, Yun-lung, and Tai-shen could do but limp home, panting and bleeding, in the cold twilight.

Shivering, Shao-shao looked up from the courtyard gate to the family-room window, a rectangle of gold shining in the gray twilight. Inside, everyone was warm and content. He did not deserve to be with them. What would Father say? He'd say Shao-shao was foolish and should not go out on his own. He'd say he got what he deserved for gambling in the street with little hoodlums. And Shao-shao knew in his heart that Father would be right.

" 'Night," he whispered to Yun-lung. They scuttled like rats to their doorways, heads down, staying close to the walls. Shao-shao put his cold hands in his jacket pockets and leaned against his door, trembling. He felt broken pieces of the lollipop he'd bought for Li-sha. He could never give it to her now.

Shao-shao opened the front door quietly and crept into the kitchen. When Gao-ma saw him, she screamed, "Aiii-ya," and covered her mouth with her hands. Trembling, she stood and stared.

Then she dropped her hands and said firmly, "I'd better wash you up before your mother sees you." She sat him down and washed his wounds with a cloth and hot water from the kettle on the stove. When she finished, she looked at him critically, searching for any dirt or blood she might have missed. "What happened?" she asked.

"Some Middle School boys challenged us to a coin toss. They said we were cheating, but we weren't. We weren't!" The tears he had been holding back for so long now burst out in long, shuddering sobs.

Gao-ma drew a chair next to him and put her arm around him. He turned his face to her shoulder and wept. "They took the butterfly kite I bought in the Old City!"

"There, don't cry. Don't cry. You're a big boy now. Anyway, you're sure to get another kite before spring." She rose, laid out a pair of chopsticks, filled a rice bowl, ladled something warm and savory over it, and offered it to him. "Everyone's had dinner," she said. "If you take off these dirty clothes, no one will know about the fight."

Second Brother teased the story out of Shao-shao as they undressed. When Shao-shao described the attackers, Second Brother answered cheerfully, "What a pea brain you are! They're the worst bullies in the whole Middle School. You're lucky to be alive. My friends and I wouldn't have anything to do with them, even if we outnumbered them three to one."

A weight swung in the pocket of Shao-shao's pants as he hung them up. He had forgotten the book *Stranger at Shaolin,* and now it came like an unexpected gift, something to take his mind off his throbbing nose. He read until Second Brother nagged him to turn the light out.

For a long time he lay quiet in the dark. His cricket had died over a month ago. He missed its chirp, singing him to sleep. He imagined that a Shaolin monk, sometimes disguised as the beggar outside the bookstore, sometimes as the old magician, appeared in the courtyard to teach him kung fu. In his dream he brandished ten swords, threw fifty knives at once, leaped to the rooftops. He pressed his finger, hard as iron, into the spot that would paralyze a bully's arm and save Yun-lung from a beating.

And when Japanese soldiers came to question Father, he beheaded them with a single stroke.

7. The Year of the Cock
December 1944–February 1945

LIGHT SNOW FELL THAT NIGHT. AT breakfast, Father hardly glanced at his youngest son. If he noticed the bruises, he gave no sign. Shao-shao didn't have to tell Father his well-rehearsed story of tripping and banging into a door.

Father left the house as soon as he had eaten, saying to Mother, "If I'm not back by eight tonight get word to Fat Ming at the Golden Dragon." She nodded silently, her face expressionless, but the tremor around her mouth and the tension in her thick black eyebrows told him she was worried.

Mother came down into the vestibule to see Shao-shao off for school. "What happened?" she asked.

"I fell getting off the streetcar," Shao-shao stammered.

Mother gave him a searching look. He knew she didn't believe him, but all she said was, "Be more careful next time. If Father didn't have so much on his mind, he would have asked you more questions."

During the long, dark nights following the unlucky expedition, Shao-shao did his homework on the table in the family room, warmed by coals burning in a large pottery brazier. There was no heat in the rest of the house, so his bedroom was freezing.

When a cold wind blew through the window frames, Shao-shao liked to draw his chair close to the brazier and rest his stocking feet on its edge. Late at night, Radio Chungking crackled out news of Japanese victories in China and American victories in the Pacific. Chungking was nearly a thousand miles away, and sometimes the signals were garbled. But it was their only link to free China.

The Shanghai station came in strong and clear, but told them only what the Japanese wanted them to know. It announced proudly that more Japanese soldiers were coming to Shanghai, to defend it from American invasion.

Meanwhile, American bombers flew in from the west and destroyed half the city's coal supply.

After that, Ah-fong put fewer coals in the blue brazier. Yun-lung worried about his goldfish. Every morning he had to break through ice at the top of their bowl. "One morning I'll find them frozen," he told Shao-shao.

At school there was no heat at all. Students and teachers wore long wool gowns over their clothes, and sometimes coats over the gowns. The outer cover of Shao-shao's gown frayed along the bottom and got worn and dirty at the knees. Gao-ma worried that the gown itself would wear out.

Everyone complained during calligraphy practice. "My hands are stiff. The ink won't mix properly." Teacher Yang always told them to do the best they could. "Adversity reveals character," she said. Yet during the cold spell, she did not punish a single student for poor calligraphy.

The streetcars stopped running by order of the Shanghai Municipal Government. Grown-ups called it the Puppet Government. Shao-shao imagined old men in long black gowns jerking like puppets over desks in a tall building beside the Bund. Above them, Japanese soldiers pulled the strings.

Now Third Sister had to ride pedicabs to her classes at St. John's. Mother sighed as she handed out cash to pay the driver, and sighed again as she counted the roll of bills after Third Sister had gone.

Western New Year came and went; 1944 became 1945. Mother hung a new calendar on the wall of the family room and Shao-shao counted the squares. Forty-two days until the real New Year, when the Year of the Monkey would be over and the Year of the Cock would begin.

Gao-ma pressed narcissus bulbs into a bowl of pebbles set near the kitchen window. Every day she watered them. When he came home from school, Shao-shao checked to see how much they had grown.

The days went by like beats of the acrobat's drum, first slowly, deliberately, as if numb with cold, then faster and faster as days lengthened and preparations for New Year began.

When the narcissus stems stood tall and green, their tops bulging with buds, school closed. Shao-shao could feel the excitement throbbing from house to house, across the courtyard, through the crowds on Nanking Road. A stack of small red envelopes stood on Mother's bureau. Ten days until New Year!

Gao-ma measured the children's feet and cut out pieces of heavy black cotton for their new shoes. Leaning on Fourth Sister's arm, Mother led Shao-shao and Second Brother from store to store, searching for the best bargains.

"We can't afford new gowns until the war is over," she told them. "But at least we can get you new covers." Even through the wrapping paper, Shao-shao could smell the crisp, new fabric.

While Mother and Fourth Sister gathered an armful of pussy willows at the goldfish and flower shop, Shao-shao and Second Brother ran around the corner to buy firecrackers.

"Remember, now," Mother warned. "You mustn't set them off until New Year's Day. Unless you want Japs in the house." Shao-shao raced Second Brother home, trying not to think of heavy black boots on the family-room carpet, of grim dark faces, of bayonets.

Six days until New Year.

In the mornings after breakfast, Gao-ma and Ah-fong went about cleaning the whole house. They swept behind the furniture and under the carpet, they dusted the walls, they washed the windows. Excitement beat a rapid rhythm now, so rapid Shao-shao could not keep still. He played shuttlecock in the courtyard with Yun-lung and Tai-shen until he shivered with cold. Then he went to warm up in the kitchen with Gao-ma and Ah-fong. They sat at the table, laughing and joking as they stitched new shoes for the children. Like him, they were looking forward to red envelopes.

Four days until New Year.

Father came home with a bit of ham, a duck, and a basket of thousand-year eggs from Fat Ming. Brother Ma brought sausage and pickled vegetables from his family's farm outside the city.

"How did you keep this from the Japs?" Mother asked. Brother Ma only laughed and said, "My uncle knows how."

Gao-ma counted out her grocery list on her fingers: "Peanuts, candied almonds, lotus seeds, watermelon seeds, orange candy, fresh tangerines, and pears."

"Don't forget a bottle of mao-tai," Mother said. "Mr. Li will want to make his New Year toasts."

Three days to New Year.

Father dumped pocketfuls of coins in a brass bowl. When no one was looking, Shao-shao took one. Father wouldn't miss it. Shao-shao would get a lot more, as well, on New Year's Eve if he hung around the gambling table. Winners were always generous. Shao-shao was the only one in the family too young to play.

Small New Year's Eve. Two days to New Year.

Gao-ma opened the downstairs parlor to air. Mother set a spray of flowers in a dark red vase on the rosewood table. Later Shao-shao watched her peel lotus roots for the special dish they always ate on New Year's Eve. "Before the war, we had ten fragrant vegetables." Mother shook her head and smiled ruefully.

Gao-ma answered, "Now we've only got six," and shrugged her shoulders, as if to say, What can you do?

"How many guests will we have?" Shao-shao asked.

"Fewer than last year, I'm sure," Mother answered. "More people have taken off for Chungking. And the rest aren't going out as much."

"Remember New Year's here in Shanghai before the Japs started making trouble? Those were good times. Life was so peaceful then. So comfortable." She held the knife in one hand, the round dark root in the other. "Now the war's changed everything. Will it ever end?"

Shao-shao left the kitchen and bounced up the back stairs, hitting the wall with his hand. There had been more food and fun in Hong Kong, he remembered. But war or no war, there would still be red envelopes, gambling money, firecrackers, and New Year's food. He was determined to enjoy himself, not long for better times.

The morning of Big New Year's Eve, Shao-shao and Second Brother woke late, to find Father gone. They did not see him until early afternoon, when a shuttlecock carelessly hit by the youngest Shih boy almost struck him in the face as he entered the courtyard. He caught it, laughing, and hit it back with the flat of his hand.

Darkness settled even before an early supper was finished. Gao-ma and Ah-fong cleared the table, laughing and teasing each other. Father, dressed in Chinese clothes, settled in the family room to wait for First Sister. Mother returned to the kitchen, where she would spend most of the night.

Leaving his sisters to help Mother, Shao-shao ran shouting through the courtyard with the boys, ran until he dropped, panting, on his front steps, breathing cold air and the smell of New Year's cooking. All around the courtyard, first-floor windows, usually dark, blazed with light. Shadows of running boys flitted past the lighted windows like good-luck bats.

Li-sha stood close to the Chen's downstairs window, watching them. She held her baby brother in her arms. Was she waiting for a visitor, as Shao-shao was waiting for First Sister? Probably not. Her relatives lived so far away.

"Happy New Year! May you make a fortune!" First Sister's infectious laugh rang through the darkness. "Happy New Year! May you make a fortune!" Shao-shao and Second Brother replied.

Brother Ma's rumbling voice asked in mock puzzlement, "Who's here? Some beggar children? My honorable brothers-in-law would not run around the courtyard. They are good boys, inside with their parents, and they are going to get what I have in my pocket."

Shao-shao knew he was teasing, but he couldn't help pulling the sleeve of the Western suit Brother Ma wore, even on Chinese New Year. "I am Li Wu-jiang, your wife's brother," he shouted.

"Is that so? You'd better get in the house then," Brother Ma shouted back.

First Sister gripped Shao-shao's shoulder and followed him through the joyous, noisy darkness. As they put on their slippers in the vestibule, Brother Ma's laughter boomed up the stairwell. The doors of the formal dining room on the first floor stood open now, framing a round table covered with a fresh, embroidered cloth.

While Brother Ma and Second Brother pounded upstairs, Shao-shao followed First Sister into the kitchen, where Mother filled sections of a yellow porcelain platter with dates, dried lychees, and lotus seeds.

"Happy New Year, Mother." First Sister made a small bow. Gao-ma put down her chopping knife, Ah-fong stopped scrubbing a serving plate. They smoothed their aprons and turned to greet First Sister.

"Happy New Year. May you make a fortune," she said as she gave them each a red envelope. They thanked her with bows and smiles. While First Sister stayed to tell Mother about the White Russian nightclub where they planned to dance all night, Shao-shao slipped upstairs to find everyone else around the table in the family room, counting the coins Father dealt out.

Father smiled across the room at Shao-shao. "Want to play?" he asked.

Shao-shao nodded, too excited to speak. Father

wanted him to join the game. Father thought he was old enough.

He took his seat, ignoring the laughter and teasing that marked the first time he was allowed to gamble on New Year's Eve.

"Is First Sister coming or not?" Father shouted.

"Coming!" she cried from the stairs. She hurried to the empty chair beside Shao-shao. "You're going to win big tonight," she whispered in his ear. "Beginner's luck."

Father rolled the dice first. Then it was Third Sister's turn. With each roll, shouts of joy or despair rose louder, as the winners took their coins and the losers watched their piles dwindle.

Father laughed from deep in his chest. He had won the most.

When a roll of the dice cost First Sister all her money, she waved her hands in a gesture of helpless disgust. Father laughed so hard he shook the table.

"Look at him," First Sister said to the others, her eyes dancing. "He's got all the money. Is that fair, I ask you?"

"No," shouted all the brothers and sisters.

"Well, what are we going to do about it?" Quickly, she answered her own question. "Let's take it and run!"

Everyone jumped up, even Third Sister. Only Brother Ma sat still. Each child grabbed a handful of cash from Father's pile and ran. Shao-shao stood in the corner of the family room, wondering how

Father would react. He might be angry, even on New Year's Eve.

But he wasn't. He laughed all the harder, sputtering, "Is that any way to treat your father?" but his voice was warm and happy, and he called them by name, inviting them back to divide up the money and start gambling all over again.

When Shao-shao woke the next morning, the first day of the Year of the Cock, Second Brother was still asleep. Downstairs, someone moved, but no noise came from Nanking Road. All around, as far as he could hear, the city was silent. Was everybody sleeping? Were the Japanese soldiers asleep or did they stand guard, even on New Year's morning?

Feeling cold air touch his ear and cheek, Shao-shao pulled the comforter up over his head. When he heard Gao-ma and Ah-fong wish Father a Happy New Year, and Father's cheerful reply, he threw off the comforter and dressed as quickly as he could. He slid his newly covered gown over his head, wriggled his shoulders to adjust it, pulled on socks and the new shoes Gao-ma had made, smoothed his hair, and ran downstairs.

He found Mother and Father in the family room, dressed in new clothes. He dropped to his knees and touched his head to the floor, chanting a formal New Year greeting, then jumped up to receive his red envelope.

"Happy New Year, Shao-shao. May this be your

best year at school. You must study hard so you can go abroad and make lots of money," Father said.

Shao-shao stood by the window to open the envelope, telling himself not to be disappointed if he got less than last year. He knew money was tight.

When he finished counting the crisp bills, he smiled with satisfaction. Father had given him the same as last year.

Meanwhile Fourth Sister, then Third Sister, and later a sleepy Second Brother greeted their parents and received their red envelopes.

"Grandmother's here," Shao-shao announced, and everyone trooped downstairs to welcome her. In the downstairs dining room, Gao-ma and Ah-fong set out the last bits of New Year's breakfast.

As Grandmother, Second Uncle, and Cousin Wei-fun entered the vestibule, shouts of "Happy New Year" volleyed back and forth like Ping-Pong balls in a tournament. When the noise died down, Grandmother said to Mother, "I hope this year brings my eldest grandson home."

Mother looked sideways at the floor, her mouth trembling. Shao-shao always felt uncomfortable when First Brother was mentioned. Mother missed him so much, but Shao-shao did not miss him at all.

"Where is that rascal?" Uncle asked. "Always up to something."

"The Japs took him, remember?" Grandmother said to Uncle, while everyone else pretended they had not heard.

"He's probably thinking of us right now," Father

said. "Next year he's sure to be with us."

Maybe he'll be different when he comes back, Shao-shao thought. Maybe he'll be kinder.

Mother smoothed the front of her silk gown with her small, white hands. Today, she wore her gold ring as well as her jade, and it glittered in the morning light. "Come on, let's eat," she said, her hands making rapid motions directing her family to the table. But she did not smile.

Shao-shao wondered how they would feel if he were gone. Would they miss him as much as they missed First Brother? He thought Mother might, but he was not sure about Father. He wondered if Father would even notice if he disappeared.

The first guests arrived in time to join the family at breakfast. All morning, guests kept arriving, moving between the parlor and the downstairs dining room, families his mother had known since she was his age, men Father knew in business when he lived in Shanghai before the war, all smiling, exchanging greetings, bringing red envelopes for the servants and sometimes for the children.

Fat Ming appeared late in the morning. Shao-shao had never seen a Western jacket cut so big. Ming's eyes seemed to disappear in folds of fat when he smiled at Shao-shao and handed him a red envelope.

Father offered Fat Ming a tiny cup of mao-tai. After they had toasted the New Year, Fat Ming and Father retreated to a far corner of the parlor and spoke quietly. The next time Shao-shao went into the parlor, Fat Ming had gone.

"Happy New Year!" More guests trooped into the vestibule. "May you make a fortune," someone shouted, and "Good health!" An older man who looked like a scholar added quietly, "I hope the war ends this year."

Mother offered cups of tea and dried lotus seeds from the centerpiece. "These are for precious sons," she said. The word *lotus* could also mean "a son on the way," and every family wanted another boy.

Visitors kept coming and going. At lunchtime, Gao-ma and Ah-fong served up dishes that Mother had cooked. When Shao-shao could not hold another grain of rice, he went to the window to watch New Year's visitors cross the courtyard, coming and going from every house. Every house but Li-sha's.

Li-sha stood on her front steps, holding her baby brother on her hip. He sucked his finger and stared wide-eyed at the people passing. Though she wore a new blue silk tunic and trousers embroidered with flowers, her face looked sad.

In the vestibule, his parents said good-bye to the An family. Only Grandmother was left at the table to see Shao-shao scoop a handful of candy from the centerpiece and stuff it in his pocket. She smiled benignly.

Shao-shao greeted the next group of visitors hastily and slipped out the front door. For the moment, the courtyard was empty. He ran toward Li-sha.

"Happy New Year," he called to her.

"May you make a fortune," she answered. She looked happy to see him.

"I'm not supposed to be out," he said, which was not true. His parents didn't mind if he played in the courtyard. They just didn't want him to play with Li-sha. "Can we go to your backyard for a while?"

He headed for the courtyard gate, looking back to see Li-sha get a good grip on her baby brother and start to follow him.

"Hey, Shao-shao!" Yun-lung appeared suddenly. "Where are you going?" Without waiting for an answer, he said, "I got twenty dollars. How much did you get?"

Li-sha stood still, holding her baby brother, staring at them. Yun-lung acted as if he didn't even see her.

"I got twenty, too," Shao-shao told Yun-lung. "A lot of coins." He had never gotten coins in Hong Kong. Only bills. "And Mother took most of it."

"Let's spend some before they take it all." Yun-lung ran out the gate.

Shao-shao hesitated, gathering his courage. "I'll come to your yard later," he told Li-sha in a loud whisper. "I have something to give you." Then he turned, half-scared at what he had promised, and followed Yun-lung.

On Nanking Road a few shops had stayed open. While Yun-lung hefted Ping-Pong paddles, Shao-shao surveyed the fireworks. It was the smallest selection he ever remembered. Second Brother said the shopkeepers must be saving them for after the war.

At the back of a shelf, Shao-shao discovered a basket of brown clay balls. "Yun-lung," he called. "I found some mud balls."

The boys gathered them as carefully as if they were fresh eggs. Mud balls had gunpowder at the center and would explode if they were dropped.

A cold wind blew up. Late winter light, struggling all day to penetrate the clouds, now began to wane. On their way up the alley toward the courtyard gate, the boys passed a group of late callers.

"Yun-lung is here," a voice chimed, and a young woman stretched out her arm.

"Auntie!" Yun-lung was swept away into the courtyard. "See you later," he called back to Shao-shao, patting the mud balls in his pocket.

Shao-shao reached into his own pocket and touched the smooth candy wrapper.

Li-sha's yard was empty. Shao-shao thrust his hands deep in his pockets and waited.

He was just about to leave when she came out the back door. She had put on a brand-new padded silk gown. Shao-shao went up to her but kept silent. She had come as he asked, but now he did not know what to say. She probably had much nicer candy inside.

"What did you buy?" she asked.

"Mud balls." He looked down at his feet, scuffing his shoe on the paving stone. Inside his pocket, his right hand gathered pieces of candy. Quickly, he scooped them up and offered them to her.

"What is it?"

"Candy."

"For me?"

Shao-shao nodded.

94

Li-sha held out her cupped hands. Shao-shao dropped the candy into them. He dared a quick glance at her face. He had to know if she was pleased or thought he was silly.

Her eyes shone. Her smile was genuine. "Thank you, Shao-shao. Orange is my favorite, but First Brother always gets first choice so he eats most of it."

"You're welcome." Shao-shao could not bring himself to speak up. "We have a lot of these."

"Papa's going to fire shooting stars later. Want to come and see?"

Shao-shao shook his head. "I said I'd shoot firecrackers with Yun-lung. We heard the Japs—Japanese—will turn a deaf ear tonight."

"They wouldn't do anything to you even if they came here," Li-sha said. "I'll tell them you're my friend."

A cold stone of fear dropped from Shao-shao's throat to the pit of his stomach. What if Mr. Chen found out about Father and Fat Ming, about the messages Third Sister copied in tiny characters?

"Don't tell them anything about me," he said, and turned and ran out along the alley, through the courtyard gate, and home.

More people were in the courtyard tonight. Tai-shen had brought his older brother, and two classmates of Second Brother's showed up. The Shih boys had five or six cousins, all elementary-school age.

"Hey, Chung," Tak-ming called Second Brother. "Want to fight?"

"Middle School against Elementary," Second Brother shouted back.

"No fair!" Shao-shao yelled.

"You've got more people, so it's fair," Tak-ming called back.

Even while they argued, they split into teams. The Shih brothers and all their cousins gathered with Shao-shao, Yun-lung, and Tai-shen in front of the Lis' doorway. The bigger boys, Tak-ming, Second Brother, and Yao-san, on the other side of the courtyard, were a clump of shadows against the Chows' lighted window.

Shao-shao reached into his pocket for a mud ball, but the older boys were quicker. A flash and a bang at their feet caused the younger boys to scatter, yelling and throwing mud balls across the courtyard. Wherever a mud ball slammed against dirt or stone, it exploded. Lighted strings of firecrackers arched through the darkness. Noise and smoke filled the courtyard.

Throwing, dodging, inviting danger, dancing with fear, Shao-shao spun through the darkness, reveling in the noise, the sound of destruction. The mud balls could be hand grenades, thrown into enemy lines; the firecrackers machine guns, throbbing out bullets; and he could be a soldier, possessing power far greater than any make-believe Shaolin monk.

Too soon, his pockets were empty, his power gone. The Shih brothers cowered in their doorway; Yun-lung had slipped on a string of spent firecrackers and sat laughing in the dirt.

96

"Hey, stop," Tai-shen called. "We're all out."

"Do you know how much noise you made?" Gao-ma called from the front door. "Do you want the Japs as New Year's guests?" They dared not ignore her vehement gesture, beckoning them in. She spoke more softly as Second Brother and Shao-shao passed close to her. "You've certainly scared away the demon spirits. Now it's time for bed."

8. The Bird
March 1945

JUST AFTER THE NEW YEAR HOLIDAY,
Yun-lung's goldfish developed black spots, turned
belly up, and died. Yun-lung blamed the cold weather
and decided not to replace them until winter was
over. He eyed the fish in the neighborhood pet store
with contempt. "They're so small and ordinary," he
complained.

Shao-shao's crickets had all died, and Gao-ma had
thrown away his dried-up silkworm eggs. Shao-shao
needed a pet. First Brother had goldfish when they
lived in Hong Kong, and Shao-shao liked to watch
them, though First Brother would not let him touch
their bowl. With his leftover New Year's money, he
could buy at least two goldfish of his own.

The Saturday before Ching-ming, the day to remember ancestors, Yun-lung and Shao-shao spent
their free afternoon walking through a warm, damp
wind to the best pet store they knew, close to the

outer edge of the French Sector. They passed a Japanese checkpoint but kept their heads down and passed unchallenged.

The shop was dark and smelled of mice and birdseed. Parents and children crowded together in the narrow aisles, peering into the closely stacked cages and tanks at turtles, white mice, goldfish, and birds. Shao-shao watched enviously as a father helped his son choose a goldfish from several drifting around a submerged pagoda.

Yun-lung intended to make a thorough study of every fish tank before he selected his new pair. Shaoshao, not so particular, wanted to see the other animals. Homing pigeons clustered in a large coop, cooing and shifting on their bamboo perch. Tai-shen kept homing pigeons on his roof, but when Second Brother had wanted some last winter, Father would not hear of it. He quoted Buddhist scripture, saying it was wrong to confine birds. They should fly free. Shao-shao suspected Father probably just didn't want a bunch of messy pigeons on his veranda.

Near the pigeon coops, bright-feathered birds perched on a bamboo pole. One sat apart from the others, its feathers iridescent blue. It cocked its head and turned a bright black eye at Shao-shao. Shaoshao puckered his lips and chirped at it. It moved toward him as if it understood, stretching its tether.

Slowly, shyly, Shao-shao touched the smooth feathers. Though its beak was a formidable weapon, heavy and pointed, the bird made no move to peck him. It seemed to welcome his touch, as if it had longed for attention and affection and he was the first person to notice it.

The shopkeeper approached. The bird was unusual, he said, and very intelligent. Its call was pleasant and soft. Shao-shao listened, trying not to show too much interest, putting in a question or two with grown-up detachment. At last he dared to ask, "How much?"

As soon as he heard the price, Shao-shao turned away. The bird cost more than the two goldfish and a bowl he had planned to buy. Unless he could bargain the man down, he would have to forget about the bird.

Hoping against hope, he looked at his feet and mumbled, "Sorry, I don't have enough for the bird, let alone the seed."

Before the shopkeeper could answer, Yun-lung called, "Hey, Shao-shao, come see what I chose."

Shao-shao could not concentrate on goldfish. Although he nodded his approval, he wasn't quite sure which ones Yun-lung had picked until the shopkeeper dipped them out into the pottery carrying jar. After the man dropped Yun-lung's coins in his cash box, he turned to Shao-shao.

"How much do you have?" he asked.

Shao-shao told him.

"Since the bird seems to like you, I'll give it to you for that, and throw in a bag of seed," he said. "I'll have to shut the shop if the war goes on much longer."

100

"Good deal!" Yun-lung punched his arm.

Speechless with joy, Shao-shao watched the shopkeeper tether the bird to a thin bamboo stick. When he grasped the stick, the bird shifted its feet to adjust its balance as if that was where it had always wanted to be. Its living warmth throbbed and quivered through the stick to his hand and his body. Silkworms, crickets, even goldfish seemed unimportant now. They didn't care who owned them, as long as they were fed. But this bird knew him, liked him, needed him, trusted him. It was his.

"What will your father say?" Yun-lung asked as they left the shop. Shao-shao slid the bird under his coat to protect it from the wind.

"Nothing. He won't know."

The storeroom beside the landing at the turn of the stairs would be a perfect place to hide the bird. Shaoshao knew how to swing the door so it would not squeak. Inside the room he navigated between chests of out-of-season clothes to a far corner. There he rigged a perch by setting a bamboo pole across the open side of a shallow wooden crate.

While the bird settled down contentedly, Shaoshao searched the house for newspaper to line the crate, string for a longer tether, and two old teacups to hold water and birdseed. When he had given the bird all it needed, he sat on the floor, enclosed by silence and the shadowy light, watching the bird.

It hopped from its perch and plunged its beak into the seed cup as if it had lived all its life in Shao-shao's house. It cracked the seeds in its beak, nodding at Shao-shao to thank him for the food.

Footsteps on the landing. Could Father have come home early? Shao-shao jumped up, cracking his head on the low ceiling. The door behind him opened.

Gao-ma sighed loudly. "You know what your father will say about this," she said. "You know he's against keeping birds."

Shao-shao put a hand over her mouth. "The bird likes me," he whispered. "It's safe here. It's tame and very intelligent. The man at the pet store told me it could be trained to do tricks."

"Your father's not going to like this." She spoke more softly, staring at the bird and shaking her head.

"He'll never find out if you don't tell him. I'll keep the bird here. He'll never see it, so he won't be angry. Please, you won't tell him, will you?"

"He'll find out sooner or later," Gao-ma grumbled, "and then you'll be in trouble." Stooping, she backed out of the room. "You'd better keep this door closed," she called softly from the landing, "or the cats will get in."

Early next morning, Shao-shao awoke with a start, thinking of the bird. Had it been frightened, all alone in the storage room? Did it have enough to eat and drink?

Second Brother breathed long and deeply, fast asleep. No noise came from downstairs. This Sunday, everyone was sleeping late. Shao-shao was too excited to go back to sleep.

He contained his excitement until Mother, Father,

and Third Sister left for Grandmother's house and Second Brother went out with friends. As soon as they were gone, Shao-shao headed straight to the storage room.

From the shadows came a welcoming chirp. He crouched silently, waiting until he could see. The bird turned its head sideways and regarded him calmly. Its seed and water were almost gone.

Carrying a broom and teacup of water from the kitchen, Shao-shao met Fourth Sister. "What's happening?" she asked.

She would find out sooner or later. If he lied to her now he would only make her angry, and he was going to need the whole family's help to keep the bird a secret from Father.

He beckoned, smiling mysteriously. She followed him into the storage room.

"Oh, it's beautiful! Where did you get it? What's its name?"

"At the pet store on the Avenue Joffre. I just call it Bird."

"Will it peck me?"

"No." Shao-shao swept up the spilled seed. "It's very tame and trusting. It's not afraid, you see."

They watched the bird eat and drink. After a while, Fourth Sister asked, "What would happen if you untied it?"

"Let's see." Shao-shao checked the door to be sure it was closed, then untied the string. The bird took a tentative hop toward them and then another. It lifted its wings and flew to a chest across the room to preen.

"It looks very pleased with itself." Fourth Sister smiled.

Shao-shao put a pinch of seeds in the palm of his hand and stretched out his arm, whistling softly. The bird cocked its head at Shao-shao, seemed to think for a moment, then swooped down to rest on Shao-shao's sleeve. It looked cautiously at Shao-shao's palm.

It took the seed with quick, gentle pecks that hurt no more than the tap of a brush handle.

When his palm was empty, Shao-shao turned his hand, feeling the little feet cling to his arm for balance. He walked slowly around the room. The bird seemed to enjoy riding on his wrist. Fourth Sister begged a turn. She had made several trips around the storage room, carrying the bird, when Shao-shao said, "Put it back on its perch and see if it will come to me again."

The bird flew to Shao-shao's wrist over and over. It was so well-behaved that they decided to take it up to the family room to give it more space. There it swooped happily from the back of a chair to the top of the high, carved chest, from there to the windowsill and back to the chair. It flew to Shao-shao's wrist when he whistled. Gao-ma, who had come to tidy up, stood still, watching the bird, open mouthed and smiling.

All next week, Shao-shao had trouble concentrating on his lessons. He couldn't do his math problems because he missed the explanation. He listened to

Teacher Yu speak for twenty minutes without understanding a word he said. All Shao-shao could think of was the bird. Was it lonely? Did it have enough water? Enough seed? What would happen if Mother found it in the storeroom? Would she keep his secret? What if Father found it? What then?

Every day he raced home to find the bird perched in the shadows, safe and secret.

Spring came all at once the day before Chingming. A cold rain blew away in the night, leaving blue skies and soft warm air in its wake. Shao-shao left Yun-lung and Tai-shen at the pet store near school and ran straight home.

Li-sha called him as he passed her fancy iron gate. He did not mean to stop, but when he looked through the grille, he saw a cage hanging beside her front door. She had brought her birds out to enjoy the warm spring air.

"Come see my birds, Shao-shao," she called.

Shao-shao pulled himself up short and leaned against the iron lotus stems. In the cage beside her, he could see fluttering green wings.

"Not now. I have to go home and check on mine."

"*You* have a bird? When did you get it?"

"Last weekend, at the big pet store on Avenue Joffre. I have to keep it in the storeroom under the stairs, because my father doesn't know about it yet. I have to go home and make sure it's all right. It's waiting for me."

"Can you bring it outside? I want to see it!"

"Maybe. It hasn't been outside yet."

"Then it should get some air, like mine."

"Sure. If my father's not home, I'll bring it."

No one was home but Gao-ma and Ah-fong, busy cooking for Ching-ming. In the storeroom a familiar chirp welcomed him.

"Here you are, here's your seed." Shao-shao untied the bird's tether and took away the pole. The bird ate from the floor, then fluttered to the top of a storage chest and looked expectantly at Shao-shao. He waved the pole up and down, calling the bird with a whistling chirp. It swooped to the pole.

"Good bird! You did it again! How about some fresh air for a reward? Now stand still, that's good, and let me tie you up again. If you fly away outside, you could get lost."

Slowly, carefully, Shao-shao descended the stairs and maneuvered pole and bird through the front door. He stood on the front steps for a moment to see what the bird would do. It shifted from one foot to another and surveyed the empty courtyard.

Yun-lung would take his time coming home. Second Brother had a Ping-Pong tournament that would keep him at school until after dark. No one was likely to catch Shao-shao visiting Li-sha.

When she saw him, Li-sha ran to open the gate. "It's so big," she said. "No wonder you don't have a cage for it."

"My bird doesn't need a cage. It lives in our storeroom."

"Can I hold it?"

"Be careful. It's heavy!"

Li-sha took the pole. "What a pretty bird you are. Would you like to meet some friends?" She carried the bird toward the cage hanging by her back door. "Say 'Hello,' " she said, holding the pole so the birds could see each other. "Say 'How are you?' "

The birds ignored each other.

Li-sha sighed. "They have no manners."

Shao-shao came close to look at Li-sha's pretty green parakeets. Their bills seemed to be carved from antique ivory. "Maybe they're shy," he said. He took the pole from her and moved the bird around to the other side of the cage. Still they all acted as if they didn't see each other. Li-sha turned away from the cage, making a pouting mouth.

"Your bird's a snob," she complained.

"He is not! He's very friendly to me!"

The bird shifted on its feet, turned its eye to look at Li-sha, and chirped.

"See?" said Shao-shao. "It's saying hello to you."

"Li-sha?" Mr. Chen's voice came from behind them. They turned to see him leaning out the back window. His shirtsleeves were rolled up, and his arms were crossed on the sill.

"Papa! Shao-shao brought his bird to visit mine, but they won't speak to each other."

Mr. Chen laughed comfortably. "Maybe they don't speak the same language." He pursed his lips and chirped at Shao-shao's bird. It cocked its head and stared at him. "What a handsome bird! Did you leave its cage at home?"

When Shao-shao hesitated, Li-sha answered for him. "It doesn't have a cage. It lives in a storeroom."

"Better get one," Mr. Chen said. He spoke kindly, as if he really cared about Shao-shao. "If the bird flies away, you'll be sad." He stretched his arms and moved back inside. "Don't keep your birds out too long, Li-sha," he said. "It will be colder soon, and you don't want them to catch a chill."

Yun-lung could be coming up the alley any time now.

"I'd better get my bird home," Shao-shao said.

"It's not that late. Would you like to see my new kite?"

"Not now. Maybe when you fly it."

Shouts came from the next street. Yun-lung and Tai-shen, playing air raid.

Shao-shao jumped up. "I'd better go." He made the first excuse that popped into his head. "I have to get ready for Ching-ming," although he had no preparations to make. He reached the street just as Yun-lung and Tai-shen turned the corner.

They ran toward him, causing the bird to flutter anxiously. "You brought your bird out," Tai-shen cried. At the same time Yun-lung asked, "Has your father found out about it?"

Li-sha watched from between two iron lotus stems. They ignored her as completely as the birds had ignored each other.

"What can it do?" Tai-shen asked. "Can it sing?"

108

Holding fast to the pole, Shao-shao walked as quickly as he could toward the courtyard. "I taught it a trick," he said. "It flies to the pole when I move it up and down. It's very smart."

"You don't even call it? You just shake the pole?" Yun-lung was incredulous.

"Let's see!" Tai-shen challenged.

Shao-shao looked from the evening sky to the bird on its pole. It watched him closely. Would it fly away, or would it come to him? All at once, he had to find out.

"You take it, Tai-shen." Shao-shao coaxed the bird off the pole. While Tai-shen spoke to the bird encouragingly in pigeon language, Shao-shao untied its leg. It was free. It could fly away. But it stayed on Tai-shen's wrist.

Out of the corner of his eye, Shao-shao saw Li-sha standing near her front window.

Shao-shao backed away slowly, holding the pole, never taking his eyes off the bird. It raised its wings slightly and uttered small, protesting chirps. After ten steps, Shao-shao stood still and slowly shook the pole.

The bird cocked its head. Shao-shao could hear the Chens' nurse singing to Li-sha's baby brother.

With a quick swoop, the bird flew to the pole.

Yun-lung clapped his hands and cheered. "I want to hold the bird," he cried. Shao-shao had just given it to him when Third Sister came into the courtyard.

"What a pretty bird! When did you get it, Yun-lung?"

109

Yun-lung looked to Shao-shao for guidance.

"He got it a couple of weeks ago," Shao-shao said in a rush.

"Better put it back in its cage," she advised as she headed home. "It might fly away."

Standing close to his house where he could not be seen from the family-room window, Shao-shao tucked the bird under his jacket. He tiptoed inside, his heart pounding. No one saw him enter the storage room.

When he joined the family, Third Sister looked at him intently, but said only, "Be sure to take your raincoat to school tomorrow. Looks like we'll have rain on Ching-ming."

Shao-shao knew that he could not keep the bird a secret from his parents forever. Surely when Father saw how smart the bird was, how happy it was with its crate and perch, how tame it was, how much Shao-shao loved it, and how well he cared for it, he would let it stay. Surely he would.

9. An Act of Charity
April 1945

BEFORE BREAKFAST THE NEXT MORNING, Third Sister held Shao-shao back on the upstairs landing. "Don't get too fond of the bird," she whispered in his ear. "Father's bound to find out eventually."

Shao-shao stared at the wooden stair tread. She must have gotten the truth out of Fourth Sister.

"The bird belongs to Yun-lung," he mumbled and ran downstairs. But he could not meet Third Sister's eyes across the breakfast table, and all through the morning, as an opaque curtain of rain sluiced across the classroom window, he worried. The patter of raindrops, the droning recitation of multiplication tables, the click of abacuses weighed his spirit down.

Nothing could penetrate his dread, not even the thought of Ching-ming lunch, not the solid heft of his fountain pen as it glided across the paper, not hearing Li-sha giggle with another girl between classes. He kept asking himself the same question, over and over.

What would Father do if he found the bird?

At last the lunch bell rang and everyone rushed to the coatroom, eager to go home. Shao-shao slipped his rubbers over his shoes and sloshed head down with the others through puddles in the school yard. Gao-ma waited under a large black umbrella outside the school gate.

Third Sister greeted them at the door and led them into the stale dimness of the downstairs parlor, where Mother and Father waited. Now Shao-shao must wait with them until Second Brother and Fourth Sister arrived from Middle School.

Shao-shao glanced furtively at Father, then looked away quickly, swallowing a lurch of fear at the grim, stony expression on Father's face.

Perhaps he's remembering Grandfather, Shao-shao told himself as he examined the border of flowers on the blue Peking carpet. Father always said he was grateful to the man who adopted him and gave him the name Li. Shao-shao did not look at Father again. The carved wooden ornaments that usually hung on the living-room wall were gone and in their place hung a photograph of Father's foster father.

The old man had a kindly expression, quite different from Father's. A wispy gray beard hung from his chin, and his hair was pulled back into a queue, the long braid Chinese men were forced to wear in the days of the Manchu emperors.

A table stood under the photograph. Gao-ma and Ah-fong had pushed the rest of the furniture against

112

the opposite wall. Incense sticks bristled like long pins from their bed of ashes in a bronze bowl under Grandfather's picture. A cushion rested on the floor in front of the table. Smoke from the burning incense sticks floated, pale blue, across Grandfather's photograph and up toward the ceiling.

Second Brother and Fourth Sister came in with a breath of damp air and a clatter of umbrellas on the tiles of the vestibule. Second Brother took his place beside Shao-shao, panting, the bottoms of his trousers dark with rain.

Now that the family was complete, Gao-ma and Ah-fong brought dishes of food for Grandfather. They set out steaming rice, pork and vegetables, dofu and mushrooms, then took their places behind the children.

While everyone stood quiet, looking at the photograph, Father stepped forward to kneel on the cushion and touch his head to the floor in front of the table. Shao-shao stared at the dirty, pitted soles of his father's Western shoes, feeling empty. He felt no respect for Grandfather. Only dread. Why did Father have to be so strict? Why couldn't he be like Li-sha's father? He didn't only *let* his daughter keep birds— he liked them, too.

When Father rose, Mother knelt on the cushion to pay her respects to Grandfather. Third Sister followed, then Second Brother, Fourth Sister, and Shao-shao. Gao-ma and Ah-fong knelt last, and when they finished, they took the food back to the kitchen, where it would be thrown away. No one could eat it, because it had been given to Grandfather.

"Now, who wants to grow up tall?" Father asked. "I do, I do," Shao-shao cried, trying to make himself heard above Second Brother and Fourth Sister. He was too old to believe that he would magically grow tall if he replaced furniture after a ceremony. But he wanted to please Father.

Shao-shao lagged behind the others as they followed their parents upstairs to lunch. He felt Father's anger coming on, heavy as an impending typhoon. Shao-shao watched his brother and sisters study their rice bowls. Gao-ma set the dishes in the center of the table and hurried down the back stairs, her eyes on the floor.

Only Father looked Shao-shao straight in the eye. "Shao-shao," he said, his voice stern, his eyebrows tight. "Today I went to the storage room to get Grandfather's photograph. Do you know what I found there?"

Shao-shao put down his chopsticks and stared at the table, his stomach churning.

"You have been keeping a bird there, caged in that dark room, a wild bird that should fly free."

"It's not in a cage!" Shao-shao felt as if a great wave had broken inside him, a rush of anger he could not control. Anger he did not want to control. "It's not wild, it's tame. It likes living in the house."

Red fury spread across Father's face. His mouth tightened, his words exploded like bullets from a ma-

114

chine gun. "Keeping a wild bird is cruel," he said. "I will not allow it in my house. Today of all days! When we get back from the temple, you must take it to the roof and let it go."

Desperate, Shao-shao turned to his mother. "I take good care of it. It will never be hungry or cold. It likes me; it does not want to leave," he cried.

Mother stared down at her hands, twisting helplessly, and said nothing.

"It was tame when I bought it," Shao-shao pleaded, trying to hold back his tears. "It cannot live on its own."

Father rose and threw his crumpled napkin on the table, alien and powerful in his Western suit. He pointed a commanding finger at Shao-shao. "Tonight, you must set the bird free."

Shao-shao moved through school that afternoon as if he were in an iron cocoon, suffocating in misery. When Teacher Yang called on him to recite, he could not speak. When she smacked his hand, the pain was nothing compared to what he felt inside.

Yun-lung's servant came for them after school, to make sure they did not linger on the way home. Shao-shao trudged silently beside Yun-lung, shivering in the chill rain. How could the bird, sheltered all its life, survive in the cold, wet city?

At home he waited in the vestibule until Gao-ma arrived with Second Brother and Fourth Sister. Grandmother hobbled downstairs. Mother helped her put on her coat while Father stood back, aloof and grim. He said nothing about the bird. As Mother and Grandmother found their umbrellas and checked to make sure they had brought matches, he spit out a command to hurry. Shao-shao longed to stay home with the bird, but knew better than to ask.

Third Sister took the three younger children with her in a pedicab. Shao-shao squeezed beside her. A metal rib of the pedicab's folding top pressed hard against his shoulder. When they reached the temple, the rain had softened to a drizzle. Ragged sheets of mist hung over a line of umbrellas winding across the temple courtyard.

On either side of the great door, two giant warriors stood, muscles bulging on their carved wooden arms and legs, swords in their hands, fearsome expressions on their faces. They protected the temple from evil spirits.

Shao-shao knew he ought to pray for his honorable ancestors to be reborn into a good life, not as animals or poor peasants, but as healthy boys in good families. Today of all days, he should think of his ancestors.

He could not. He could only think of his bird.

He huddled between Grandmother and Mother, sheltered by Mother's umbrella. There, among all those people on this solemn occasion, he could not speak as he would at home. He could not beg Mother to ask Father to change his mind. Grandmother balanced herself on his shoulder as the line moved forward. Would she scold him if she knew he could not pray for his ancestors, for Second Sister who had died so young?

116

At last they passed the guardian warriors and walked into darkness thick with the smell of incense. Grandmother and Mother bought long sticks of incense from a monk at the doorway. Father struck a match to light them. The incense caught fire and burned without a flame, giving off a warm sweet smoke that would rise to heaven.

Shao-shao carried his stick through a maze of carved wooden screens. From behind one screen, monks chanted, striking wooden clappers to punctuate their prayers. Someone wealthy had paid the monks to pray for his ancestors.

Images of Buddha lined the walls, far up into the dark, smoky heights. A babble of prayers rose from the altar they could not yet see. Shao-shao felt removed from it all, in his own private world of pain and fear, a world no one else could enter.

The line inched forward. At last they saw the kind and benevolent Buddha presiding over the altar. Incense sticks bristled from the sand filling a huge bronze urn beside the altar. Shao-shao pushed forward and tried to whisper a proper prayer. But the voice of his heart begged, *Please make Father change his mind,* although he knew Buddha would not hear him.

Their pedicab drivers met them at the other side of the temple. As they rode home, thoughtful and silent, the clouds blew apart, revealing patches of blue sky.

Now I can't even ask Father to let me wait until the rain stops, Shao-shao thought glumly.

117

When he crept into the storage room, the bird greeted him with a cocked head and cheery bright eye. It clung to his sleeve as he gathered a bag of seed and mounted the stairs to the roof. Everyone ignored Shao-shao as he passed the family-room door with the bird held against his chest. He was glad. He did not want anyone to see him crying.

He spread the seeds along the veranda railing and eased the bird to perch beside them. The bird pecked the seeds and eyed Shao-shao, as if it intended to stay put on the veranda railing, as if it could not imagine flying through open air.

Shao-shao waved at it, but still it did not move. He lifted it to his sleeve once more, allowing his tears to spill out, for no one could see or hear him but the bird.

"Oh, Bird, please forgive me. I hope you'll find another home, where someone will love you as much. . . ."

He lifted his arm quickly and threw the bird into the air. It flew away, feathers flashing blue in the afternoon sun, to land on a neighboring rooftop. He kept his eyes on the distant speck of blue until it was too dark to see anymore.

Shao-shao went down to his bedroom and stretched out on his bed. He did not turn on a light, but lay silently in the dark. His tears were gone. He bit his lip until he tasted blood.

It seemed a lifetime passed before he heard soft, tentative footsteps on the stairs.

Mother. She switched on a painful flood of bright

118

light. "Time for dinner," she said softly.

"I don't want any." Shao-shao turned his face to the wall.

Mother sat on the bed and rubbed his shoulder. Her hands were smaller than Gao-ma's but just as strong.

"You must eat," she said, "so you'll grow big and strong. When you're a man, with a house and family of your own, you'll have all the birds you want."

She lifted him up. "Come on now. Don't sulk. Your father is only doing what he thinks is right."

At dinner, Father smiled at Shao-shao. "When you are older you will understand. Birds should not be confined. They are meant to fly free."

After dinner, Mother took him aside and put two small coins in his hand. "Buy something nice tomorrow," she whispered.

The next day after school, Shao-shao ran up the stairs. His heart thumping, he opened the veranda door just a crack and peeped through.

On the railing, eating seeds, sat the bird.

Shao-shao eased his body through the door, trembling with excitement and hope. Warmer weather was coming. The bird could live on the veranda.

He pursed his lips to call it and held out his arm. The bird fluttered, chirped, lifted its wings, and flew away. It had forgotten him.

Shao-shao went up to the veranda every day for more than a week. Though he watched and waited, sometimes as long as an hour, he never saw the bird again. A cold wind blew in from the west, bringing more rain, rain that continued for three days. How would a bird born in captivity know how to find food and shelter in the cold, rainy city? Shivering, Shao-shao scanned the rooftops, certain that the bird was dead.

Father doesn't really care about the bird, Shao-shao told himself bitterly. He doesn't even care about me. He only cares about himself and how righteous he feels after this act of charity.

10. A Wind for Kites
April 1945

THOUGH NO ONE TOLD HIM SO, SHAO-
shao knew that Father was doing something danger-
ous with Fat Ming and his underground network.
Father was gone more often these days, and it was
hard to get Mother's attention while she waited for
him. Third Sister never failed to ask about Father
when she came home from St. John's. She tried to
sound casual, but Shao-shao could tell she was
worried.

Shao-shao knew that Father was probably doing
something brave, something admirable. Yet his anger
at Father remained like a lump of twisted shrapnel
embedded in his flesh. He could not bring himself to
look at Father or speak to him. If Father knew of
Shao-shao's feelings he gave no sign. He was too
preoccupied to pay attention to his youngest son.

One afternoon when Third Sister came home from
St. John's, she said she had seen American planes
flying low over the northern suburbs, strafing the

barracks where Japanese soldiers lived.

"They'll land here after they've finished in Europe," Second Brother predicted. "It won't be long before they take the Philippines."

"If the Americans come, the Japs will destroy the city." Mother turned from where she sat by the window, waiting for Father.

"They wouldn't do that," Third Sister said.

"That's what they said they'd do. They don't make idle threats."

Shao-shao still went up to the veranda every day, but the bird did not return. What would happen to his bird if the Japanese destroyed Shanghai?

Yun-lung and Tai-shen did not worry about battles or lost pets. On the way home from school these days, they talked of nothing but kites. They hoped for windy weather after weeks of rain or still, overcast days. Shao-shao trudged behind them. Once, long ago, he had been excited about kite flying. The memory seemed as far away as his years in Hong Kong. He had been a carefree baby then.

At home he trudged upstairs, dropped his books on his bed, and started toward the veranda. He stopped, looking at the kites leaning against the wall behind his door. Third Sister had brought them with her when she came home from St. John's the day after Ching-ming. One was plain, for him to decorate. The other was shaped like a butterfly. Had she found out about the butterfly kite the bullies had stolen? Shao-shao didn't dare ask.

Shao-shao's hand stretched listlessly toward the plain kite. He would have to fix it up sometime. He rummaged through his dresser drawers for a spool of kite string. When he found the string, he tied it on and hefted the kite for balance.

A few minutes later he was in the kitchen asking Gao-ma to give him some rags. She didn't ask him why he wanted them. She put down her large knife and quickly pulled a handful of rags out of a basket. "Get along upstairs and stay there!" she told him. "I'm busy."

He tore the rags into strips and knotted them together for the tail. When the kite balanced perfectly, he mixed some ink and wrote in his biggest brush from top to bottom, "May all things come my way."

He held up the kite, admiring his work. Satisfaction felt like a gold coin lost and found again. As he wiped his ink stone, he heard conversation rising up the stairwell. A stranger's voice sounded low and indistinct; his father's louder and more jovial. What was Father doing home at this time of day? Shao-shao went out on the landing and listened. He could hear that the stranger and Father stood on the landing beside the storage room.

"Of course you'll be safe." That was Father's voice, hearty, reassuring.

Shao-shao could not make out the stranger's answer.

"They patrol the streets, sure. They've never come into the courtyard."

Another weak murmur.

"If they find out, they're old enough to keep their mouths shut."

Shao-shao gasped for breath, as if he had been socked in the stomach. He heard the familiar sound of the storage-room door opening. It squeaked if you didn't swing it a certain way. Then shuffling. Again, the squeak.

Shao-shao edged silently back to his room, hoping Father had not seen him. He sat on the edge of his bed, gripping the side slats under the coverlet, trying to stop trembling.

Father ate dinner at home that night, but Mother did not seem happy to see him. She stared at her rice bowl and picked at grains with her chopsticks. Father ate his rice mechanically and held the bowl out for Ah-fong to refill. He did not even glance at her, nor did he notice Shao-shao watching him. A short time after dinner he said, "The boys should go to bed early tonight. They've been getting into bad habits lately."

Shao-shao had not finished his homework, but he did not argue. He gathered up his books and solved his last math problems sitting on his bed. Long after Gao-ma turned out the light, he lay awake, every muscle tense, listening to Second Brother's deep, rhythmic breathing.

Downstairs, he heard Father's heavy footsteps, the familiar squeak of the storage-room door, the shuffle of strange feet.

"Nothing spicy. Just some plain rice." The voice was hoarse and halting, as if speaking was an effort.

Shao-shao heard them walk into the family room.

He slipped out of bed and crept downstairs. He stopped on the fourth stair above the family-room door. Its open door cast a rectangle of light across the dark landing.

"Have some soup. It will give you strength," Father said.

Something touched his arm. Shao-shao started, turned, and found himself face-to-face with Fourth Sister. She put her finger to her lips and led him down one step, two, until they could see into the family room. The shades were drawn and the lamp was draped in air-raid black. A man hunched over the table. His clothes were shabby but clean, his hair cut so short that his scalp showed.

Gao-ma set rice and soup before the man, averting her eyes as if she did not want to see him. He ate greedily. Shao-shao noticed the prominent bones on his wrist, the tremor in his cheek.

"Eat all you want," Father said. "You must be starved."

"After a while all you think of is food. . . ."

The hoarse voice quavered and broke off. Shao-shao's throat tightened when he saw tears glittering in the man's eyes. He didn't want to hear any more. Fourth Sister followed him as he tiptoed upstairs. He lay in bed, waiting for sleep, listening to the muffled voices and the loud beating of his own heart.

The next morning, Shao-shao woke from a dream that Bird was perched on his bedpost. The hope and happiness of his dream stayed with him after he opened his eyes. He jumped from his bed and looked out the window. On Nanking Road, pale green tree-tops were waving in the wind. Wind for his kite! He wondered if the wind would blow all day and then remembered it was Saturday, a half day of school. He could fly kites in the afternoon.

Second Brother turned over and groaned.

Gao-ma opened the bedroom door. "Not up yet?" she scolded. "Hurry, or you'll be late for school."

"Gao-ma, what happened to the man Father's hiding?" Shao-shao asked.

Gao-ma threw him a quick sharp look. "Don't concern yourself with him. Just remember, there are more important things to hide in the storage room than birds."

Shao-shao bent his head over his shoes to keep himself from yelling back at her.

"He escaped from the Japs," Second Brother said. "They beat him up, but he didn't give anything away."

"Quiet!" Gao-ma whispered fiercely as she shooed them downstairs for breakfast.

All morning Shao-shao looked out the schoolroom windows to see the leaves turning their white sides up. A steady wind polished the sky until it shone bright blue.

After the last bell rang at noon, the boys found Yun-lung's servant waiting for them at the school gate. "You must come straight home," she told Yun-lung. "Your grandma's here for a visit." She wouldn't listen to Yun-lung's protests that he had planned to fly his kite. "Maybe later," was all she would promise.

At lunch, Father had a tight, worried look around his mouth. He drummed his fingers on the table, watching the family eat. "Third Sister brought you two kites," he said to Shao-shao. "When are you going to fly them?"

Shao-shao asked Second Brother, "Going kite-flying this afternoon?"

"Yes, with my friends. We're going to the British Sector, and we don't want you tagging along. You go with Yun-lung."

"He can't."

"Gao-ma will take you," Mother said quickly.

Father smiled absently. "You're sure to find friends on the field," he said.

Shao-shao guessed that Father wanted everyone out of the house because of the man he was hiding. Whatever the reason, he was glad Father was giving him a chance to have some fun. Before Gao-ma could finish her instructions to Ah-fong, he was out of the house, running across the courtyard, the painted kite flopping over his shoulder.

In the alley he caught up with Li-sha walking beside her nurse. The woman carried a kite. Li-sha did not look at him. Now that he thought of it, she had ignored his smile since the day before Ching-ming, when he'd showed her his bird. Maybe she felt bad at the way he'd ignored her when his friends came along.

"Going to fly your kite there?" he asked, waving his

arm in the direction of the open field two blocks from the house.

Li-sha nodded, not looking at him.

Behind them, Gao-ma called, "Not so fast!"

Li-sha's nurse glanced over her shoulder and turned away quickly.

Shao-shao dropped back to walk with Gao-ma.

Kites—brilliant butterflies, dragons, and tigers—bobbed against moving clouds in the sky ahead. The wind carried the scent of fried dumplings. By the time Gao-ma and Shao-shao reached the street leading to the field, Li-sha and her servant had disappeared. They might have joined the crowd around the open-air stalls surrounding the field, or they might have gone into the field to fly Li-sha's kite.

Three men ran across open grass, trying to launch a huge caterpillar kite. Its circular sections billowed as it caught the wind. A gang of children ran along beside the men, laughing and shouting encouragement. Three Japanese soldiers, in uniform but without weapons, watched the kites from the far side of the field.

Gao-ma stopped at a fruit stand. Shao-shao ran past her, into the field, searching for a clear spot. "Fly your kite high," she called after him. "Make bad spirits fly away."

The grass felt springy under Shao-shao's feet. Cool fresh air filled his lungs; laughter bubbled up inside him. He laughed at his plain kite, bouncing along behind him, because it would not rise. He laughed as he pivoted and ran back the way he had come. He

128

laughed as a gust of wind caught his kite. He planted his feet firmly on the ground and played his spool of string out, trying to make his kite rise on the current of wind.

At last the kite soared into the sky. "Bad spirits, fly away!" he shouted.

The kite rose until all Shao-shao could see was a small white shape against the blue, connected to him by a living string that tugged him upward. He imagined flying along that string to ride the wind, surveying the earth below, serene as Buddha in the temple.

A butterfly kite hit the ground beside him. Li-sha ran to pick it up. He called her name, hoping she wouldn't run away. "Can I help?" he asked.

She stood still, holding her kite. "It won't fly," she said.

"Fancy kites are hard to launch. Maybe I can do it."

"Oh, *would* you?" She smiled at last.

"Here, hold mine," he said, handing her the near-empty spool.

After several tries, Shao-shao set her kite sailing on the wind. They traded spools, but she did not run with her kite. She stayed beside him, looking up into the bright sky.

"You don't bring your bird out anymore." He could hear the gentle reproof in her voice.

"My father made me let it go. It came back to the veranda the next day, but it didn't know me. It never came back again." Shao-shao had never told anyone else, not Gao-ma, not his mother.

She glanced at him sideways. "That's too bad."

She sounded so sorry that Shao-shao looked straight at her to see if she was teasing him. No one in his family had been that sympathetic. She was not teasing. Her expression was completely sincere. "You can come and play with my birds anytime," she said.

The thought of going inside Li-sha's house made him catch his breath, as if the atmosphere of collaboration would poison him. What could happen to Father if Mr. Chen found out about the man hidden in the storage room?

He looked up to see his kite shining in the sun and thought of bayonets.

After a while he said, "I'm afraid my bird is dead. I don't see how it could survive on its own."

"It's too pretty to die," Li-sha answered matter-of-factly. "I bet someone took it in. That's why it didn't come back. I'm sure it's happy, wherever it is."

She sounded so certain that at that moment Shao-shao allowed himself to be convinced. He would never know what had happened to the bird. Why not imagine it alive? Perhaps his dream had been an omen, Bird's message telling him it was safe.

He looked at Li-sha and smiled. She really wanted to make him feel better.

They flew their kites together in a comfortable silence. Shao-shao saw Gao-ma watching them from the edge of the field. She did not call him away.

Then Yun-lung's voice came from the edge of the field.

Shao-shao jumped, ready to run. Then he stopped.

It would be rude to leave Li-sha as he had before, especially after she had been so nice to him. He could never go to her house, but that didn't mean they could not be friends. Besides, Yun-lung had already seen them together.

He waved at Yun-lung. He knew the boys would tease him, but just then he didn't care. He didn't always have to do what they wanted. He could be friends with Li-sha if he chose.

Yun-lung ran toward them, but stopped a little distance away, waiting for Shao-shao to join him. Let him wait.

After a while, he said, "Yun-lung wants me to fly a kite with him. Can you manage?"

She swallowed, stopped smiling, and looked away. He stayed beside her until she nodded.

"I'll come visit you," he called as he ran across the field, pulling his kite along. This time he meant to keep his promise, in spite of Yun-lung, in spite of Father.

A gust of joy caught him and carried his spirit up, buoyant and fearless as a kite upon the wind.

11. Cricket Songs
May 1945

ABOVE THE COURTYARD, TENDER NEW leaves unfolded and sparrows built untidy nests in the roof tiles. As the weather turned warmer, shoppers and beggars crowded the sidewalks on Nanking Road. Shao-shao never forgot his bird, but he stopped watching for it on the veranda. Instead he played marbles in the courtyard during the long spring afternoons. When the rain stopped and the air was soft and warm, how could he study inside, even though final exams were coming up?

One night when he was supposed to be changing into his pajamas, Shao-shao poked under his bed until he found his empty cricket pots. This year, he told himself, he would not give up searching until he found a really big cricket, one that could beat all the others. He had a place to look where his friends couldn't go: Li-sha's backyard. He had kept his promise and gone to visit while she aired her birds. He always found some excuse not to go inside her house, and he tried to keep his visits secret from the boys. They had teased him enough about his "traitor girlfriend" since Yun-lung had seen them flying kites together.

He ignored them. He liked talking to Li-sha. She was different from Tai-shen and Yun-lung, different from all his family. There was something soft about her, like the spring air.

Most evenings, the older members of Shao-shao's family did not notice if he cleaned his cricket pots or played marbles when he should be studying for final exams. They were too absorbed in the broadcasts from Chungking.

American soldiers had landed on the Japanese island of Okinawa, and were fighting a bloody battle to take it away from the Japanese. If they won, their bombers would have a much shorter flight to Shanghai. Meanwhile, there were great battles in faraway Europe, and the Germans were losing.

"Shao-shao, your brush is dripping," Mother warned.

A few days after Third Sister had torn the April page off the Western calendar, Shao-shao sat at the family-room table, preparing for his Chinese exam. In his notebook he had copied the five poems Teacher Yang had assigned. They would have to write at least two of them from memory, and Teacher Yang would grade equally on calligraphy and accuracy. But which two? Of course Teacher Yang would not say. She told them to study all five.

The twilight faded into darkness, and Mother pulled thin, white curtains across the open windows. It was too hot to draw the shades, unless there was a night air-raid.

Father lowered his newspaper and stared out the window. He had come home thoughtful and preoccupied, with little to say.

"What poem are you writing?" Third Sister asked.

"One by Li Po." Shao-shao read what he had written:

> *"Bright moon lights my bed*
> *Like frost upon the ground.*
> *I raise my head to see the moon*
> *Then drop back and think of home."*

Suddenly, Father turned his attention to Shao-shao. "My brother taught me that poem," he said.

Fourth Sister looked up from her homework. Third Sister turned off the radio. It was broadcasting nothing but static.

Outside, a lone cricket chirped.

Shao-shao had never heard Father mention his elder brother. Why did First Uncle never come to visit?

Third Sister seemed to read Shao-shao's thoughts. She said, "I don't think you've ever told the younger ones about your brother."

Father's eyes met Shao-shao's. "He took me with him when he ran away from our father's house," Father said, in a low voice. "He wouldn't leave me

134

where I'd be beaten or worked to death."

Father closed his paper and folded it, smoothing the folds on his lap. Abruptly, he stood up and went to the window.

"He left me in the end, though." Father spoke softly.

Shao-shao stared at Mother. She pointed to the copy sheet before him and gestured writing.

Shao-shao compared what he had written from memory with the version he had copied off the blackboard. He had not made a single mistake! And he knew he was one of the best writers in the fifth grade. He looked at Mother over the bent heads of Fourth Sister and Second Brother. Father remained by the window, looking out.

"Can I go look for a cricket?" he asked.

Before Mother could say anything, Father answered.

"No," he said sharply, the sadness in his voice gone. "You spent all afternoon playing marbles. You should spend all evening studying."

"It's not fair. Yun-lung has a cricket. So does Tai-shen. They've already had a fight. I don't have one yet."

Father turned, glowering. Shao-shao looked down, knowing he must say no more, or Father's anger would explode and everyone would suffer. The house would be so peaceful without Father, he thought. His hand shook, and he spoiled the next brush stroke as he ground anger between his teeth. He imagined that when he looked up, Father would be gone. With

135

anger came fear, fear that Father would know this shameful thought.

Mother spoke quickly, firmly. "If you come straight home from school tomorrow and study before supper, Gao-ma will take you out to find a cricket."

"You'll never find one, stupid," Second Brother said, his voice ripe with scorn. "It's too early to start cricket hunting."

Shao-shao ignored him. Yun-lung had looked a long time, but he found a cricket in the end.

The next day Shao-shao woke to a steady, warm rain. At school Yun-lung boasted about how much rice his cricket ate and how big and strong it was getting. Shao-shao longed to catch one of his own. But the rain did not stop, so all he could do was memorize his five poems and work out every problem to the end of his math book. Mother praised his calligraphy and showed it to Father, who said Shao-shao would write like a real scholar if only he'd practice.

Three days later, the rain lightened to a fine mist as the boys walked home from school. By nightfall it had ceased entirely. Shao-shao led Gao-ma out of the house into the warm night to follow scattered cricket calls. Intent on the radio, Father hardly noticed when they left.

With his flashlight and collecting tube in his pocket, Shao-shao clutched his net and walked slowly, listening to find the source of the song. Gao-ma padded after him, carrying a teakettle of cold

136

water. A sound drew him across the courtyard, to the foot of the tree.

Clear and strong, from the unpaved earth beneath his feet, a cricket chirped.

Shao-shao stopped and whispered a warning to Gao-ma. Setting his flashlight on the ground, he took the kettle from her hand. With his light shining in the direction of the sound, he lifted a large rock and poured water into the earth. A small dark body jumped up, flushed out of its burrow, dazed by the bright light.

Quickly, Shao-shao scooped the cricket into the net and covered it with his open palm to keep it from escaping while he reached for the collecting tube. He felt it bounce against his palm, prick him with its needle fangs. He slid the collecting tube into the net, but the cricket was too quick for him.

"It got away," he whispered sadly.

"Never mind, there are more," Gao-ma whispered back.

In the distance, a cricket voice called. And another. Shao-shao stood still, listening, trying to guess the direction. Then he headed for the courtyard gate, forgetting everything but the crickets' songs.

"Don't go so fast," Gao-ma panted behind him.

"You stay here," Shao-shao whispered as they stood in the alley. Before she could object, he grabbed the kettle and opened the latch of the Chens' garden gate. The iron vines were smooth and cool as he swung the gate wide and walked in. A cricket song came from beneath a stepping-stone surrounded by moss. Shao-shao turned the stone slightly and poured water around it. A large cricket struggled upward into Shao-shao's net. This time he captured it in the bamboo tube and plugged the top with cotton.

"Come back," Gao-ma called softly.

"Just one more," Shao-shao said. He stuffed the tube in his pocket and followed a chirp toward the little poplar tree in the corner of the Chens' small garden.

Just as he was locking in a second cricket, someone came up beside him. Startled, he almost dropped the bamboo tube.

"I saw you from my bedroom window." Li-sha spoke in a panting whisper, as if she had been running. "Everyone else is listening to the radio. They don't know I'm out. Have you caught any crickets?"

"Two."

"Good. I hope they're strong fighters."

"They aren't very big yet, but I'm going to feed them hot peppers to make them fierce."

"Can I see them?"

"If I open the tubes now, they'll get away. I'll show them to you when they're settled in their pots."

"Tomorrow?" Her voice was tremulous. Hearing it in the dark, Shao-shao felt guilty for keeping silent when the boys called her "traitor."

"I don't know. I have to . . ." Before he could explain about how his father wanted him to study for final exams, Gao-ma charged out of the darkness, grabbed his shoulder, and whispered sharply to Li-sha, "You should go inside at once. You know your

parents will be angry if they find you out at night."
She pulled Shao-shao back toward the courtyard.

Struggling against her grip, he called softly at Li-sha's shadow, "I'll come after supper."

After the leaf-fragrant darkness, the lights in the family room hurt Shao-shao's eyes. Nobody wanted to hear about his crickets. They were all too intent on the radio. The Germans had surrendered, and Hitler, their evil leader, was dead.

"It's all over in Europe," Third Sister said. "Now the Japs are fighting alone."

"They'll never surrender," Father predicted.

"How long can they hold out?" Mother asked, looking out the window.

Clutching the bamboo tubes tightly against his chest, Shao-shao thought, She's worrying about First Brother.

"A year at least," Father said. Then, to Mother: "We might as well tell them now."

No one spoke. They all waited for Father's announcement.

"We're going to Chungking," he said.

For a moment, everyone sat stunned into silence. Then they all talked at once.

"Chungking's dirty and too crowded," Second Brother protested.

"All my friends are in Shanghai," Fourth Sister wailed.

"Chungking's bombed all the time," Shao-shao yelled.

"Be quiet!" Mother snapped, silencing everyone.

"Do you want us to starve? Or get bombed out of Shanghai?" She leaned forward, her jade ring gleaming as her hand sliced the air. "Do you want your Father arrested?"

"Your friends will leave, too, if their parents are smart," Third Sister said to Fourth Sister. "Do you want to be all alone at school next year?"

Fourth Sister dropped her eyes and said no more.

"You children probably won't leave till the end of summer," Father said. "I have to go as soon as I can. Fat Ming's arranging a pass. That might take a month. We'll move after I've found a place."

As he spoke, Father looked at each child in turn. Shao-shao could not meet his eyes. He was afraid Father would see his joy at the thought of a whole summer to do as he pleased. A summer without Father!

"I'm sorry you won't be able to finish at St. John's," Father said to Third Sister. "But inflation is so bad we'll spend all our money before the year is out, and I couldn't afford tuition anyway."

Third Sister examined the tall carved chest and did not answer. What could any of them say? Father had decided.

The room was still for so long that Father's next words burst out like machine-gun fire. "We'd be eating watered rice now if it weren't for Fat Ming. Even his supply is running low. He says it may not last a month. Besides, have any of you thought what it might be like when the Americans land? There will be

140

shooting on the streets. The Japs will fight until they're all dead."

Third Sister shuddered and threw her arm around Fourth Sister. But she said, "Just think, no more Japanese lessons. You'll go to school in Free China."

"No Japanese lessons?" Second Brother shouted. "When do we start packing?"

While the rest of his family planned the journey, Shao-shao kept silent. He could not share the excitement swirling around him. His joy was poisoned by a bitter taste of fear.

Even the most ferocious crickets never fought to the death.

12. A Wish Granted
May–July 1945

HARD RAIN THAT BEGAN DURING SUPPER
the next day kept Shao-shao from showing Li-sha his
crickets. Then Father announced that everyone must
stay home and study for final exams. "I'm going to be
here every day until I get my pass," he said. "I'll see
that you do your work."

Every day Shao-shao would come home from
school and go into the kitchen, always hoping to hear
Gao-ma say, "Your father has gone." Long warm
evenings passed, and the cricket chorus swelled, calling to him as he sat inside studying while Father read
the paper. June went by, and he could not catch
another cricket. He could not see Li-sha, except at
school.

Father was still in Shanghai during final examination week. He opened the report cards his youngest
children brought home on their last day of school.

Father had nothing but praise for Third Sister,
because she finished fifth in her class at St. John's.

Third Brother failed his final examination in Japanese, which did not upset Father nearly so much as his low grades in other subjects. Fourth Sister's grades satisfied Father, and he smiled to read the teachers' praise for her cooperation and diligence. Shao-shao ranked in the top fourth of his class, but Father had nothing to say about that. In a loud, angry voice he read what Shao-shao's teachers had to say about his behavior. "He is smart, but too active."

Father lectured his sons over the dinner table. "You'll never amount to anything!" he thundered at them. "You, Shao-shao, are the worst. Teacher Yang says you're smart. But you won't work. You have the best opportunity in the family. You're a British subject. You can go abroad when the war's over. But you'll never have a boundless future unless you learn to work."

Shao-shao looked down at his lap. Ah-fong filled his rice bowl, but he did not touch it. It was always the same. Father never would be pleased with him, no matter what he did. As soon as dinner was over, he went to the window to see who was in the courtyard.

No one was there. Only Fourth Sister's friend Mei-ling, skipping rope beside her house. The Shihs had already gone to Chungking. Yun-lung was still at dinner.

Yun-lung's parents would reward him just for being in the top half of his class, Shao-shao thought bitterly.

Watching Mei-ling, Shao-shao thought of Li-sha skipping rope on Double Ten Day. He looked back at his family. Father and Mother were reading the newspaper, and Third Sister was talking on the telephone to Kuo Yuan-yi. "I don't think we should. That block was swarming with Japs yesterday. Some kind of defense drill. . . ."

Shao-shao slipped out of the family room. Now that exams were over, Father would not care where he went. He tiptoed downstairs, but stopped in the vestibule, turned, and mounted the stairs again. As he passed the family room, no one looked up, nor did anyone notice when he came back down again, holding his cricket pot.

He waited beside the Chens' gate as twilight seeped into the warm, heavy air. It was getting dark, and still Li-sha did not come out. He heard a man's voice rise inside the house. He imagined the Chens comfortable around their table, and Mr. Chen laughing easily.

Li-sha had never taken this long before. He would count to one hundred. If she had not come by then, he would go home. When he got to seventy-five, the back door opened a crack, and Li-sha slipped out. She walked quickly across the garden, glancing over her shoulder at the house. She stood behind the grille, but she did not open the gate or invite him in. Her face wore a new expression, angry and closed.

"Why didn't you go away?" she whispered. "Didn't you hear Papa shouting?"

He felt slow and stupid. He could not understand why she was so upset. Even her father must shout

144

once in a while. That was what fathers did.

"You got a good report card. Why is he angry?"

"He didn't even see my report card." She unlatched the gate and slipped out to lean against the wall. She still looked angry. "Our maid and cook left this morning. Only my nurse is left. Papa and Mama have been arguing all day. He doesn't go to work these days. The Japanese don't want him. Mother says now that the Americans have Okinawa, it's a matter of time before they come here. She says we should go back to Manchukuo right away."

Her words tumbled out, too fast to make sense of.

He said: "Leave? Now?" If she heard him, she gave no sign. She sounded as if she might cry.

"Papa got really mad then. He shouted at Mama. She shouted right back. I took First Brother away."

She wiped her nose with the back of her hand, fighting tears. Shao-shao did not know what to say. Every Chinese he knew was overjoyed when the Americans captured the island of Okinawa. Now that they had a base so close to China, American bombers flew over Shanghai more often. Shao-shao had lost count of the air raids he'd watched from the roof, or of the nights he'd rushed around the house, turning out lights and pulling down black-out curtains.

Things were all mixed up. Li-sha sounded like a person Shao-shao did not know, like a person he did not want to know. She had always cheered him up. Now she didn't even realize he was sad.

He wished she would be herself again. Before he

thought, he lifted his free hand to touch her shoulder but suddenly turned shy and held out his cricket pot instead.

"Want to see my cricket?" he asked.

He set the pot on the cobblestones of the street and squatted down beside it.

For a moment, she stared at him as if she did not understand. Then she eased down beside him and peered into the jar.

"I don't see it," she pouted.

Shao-shao looked. "He's sleeping," he said. He reached into the pot and shook the cricket out of its tiny house, holding the lid ready in case it should jump.

"There he is!" Li-sha said. They watched as the cricket nibbled on the grains of rice.

"He likes hot peppers, too." Shao-shao pulled a frayed stem of grass from his pocket and tickled the cricket with it. "See how fast he puts out his fangs?"

Li-sha almost smiled. She looked more like the person he knew. "Can I try?" she asked.

He handed her the stem of grass. Gingerly she touched the cricket's head with the frayed end. The cricket spread his fangs.

"Ready to fight, are you?" Li-sha said. She sounded like herself, too.

He wanted to tell her that he, too, might be leaving. But he knew he must not. Mr. Chen must not know Father's plans.

With a harsh, abrupt shout, Mr. Chen called Li-sha into the house.

146

"I have to go," she said. "It's First Brother's bedtime. Mama says I have to take care of him now that Nurse has no helpers."

Shao-shao leaned against the iron lotus stems and watched her through the gate as she plodded toward her back door, shoulders slumped, head down.

He never thought Li-sha would hate to go home when her father was there. He wanted to call out to her, to say something that would make her feel better, but she went inside before he could open his mouth.

Two days later, as she laid out Shao-shao's breakfast, Gao-ma told him the news he had waited so long to hear. A message had come from Fat Ming at dawn. Father's travel papers were ready. He must leave in the afternoon. Brother Ma would see him to the station.

"You take good care of the children," he told Mother when they all said good-bye.

Shao-shao bowed with his brothers and sisters and wished Father a safe journey. He looked at the floor, hoping no one could see the happiness in his heart. He had gotten his wish at last. Father was leaving. He hoped Father would be gone for a long time.

The family watched from the window as Father and Brother Ma crossed the courtyard. Shao-shao thought Father looked like an old-fashioned shopkeeper in his long Chinese gown. Mother murmured a prayer as they passed through the gateway.

"Where will he sleep tonight?" Third Sister asked.

"In Hangchow," Mother answered. "He'll stay

with friends he knew before we were married."

Shao-shao had heard that story many times. Father saw Mother through the window of her family's shop and sent the matchmaker there the next day.

"He always looks sad when he speaks of Hangchow," Third Sister said. Her shoulders slumped, as if she had lost her spirit.

She's really sorry to see Father go, Shao-shao thought.

"That's because of First Uncle," Mother said softly.

Shao-shao turned away from the window to stare at Mother. Fourth Sister looked surprised and curious, too, for Mother used the word that meant "father's brother." The mysterious Uncle that Father had mentioned the day Shao-shao recited the poem.

"Where is First Uncle now?" he asked.

Mother raised her hand toward her throat and quickly reached back to smooth her hair. Third Sister opened her mouth to speak, looking from Mother to Shao-shao as if she could not decide what to say.

Mother finally broke the silence. "He's dead, Shao-shao. He died of tuberculosis when Father was thirteen."

"You must never speak of him to Father," Third Sister said quickly. Her eyes glittered with tears.

Down in the courtyard, Mei-ling chanted a jump-rope rhyme. In the family room, everyone was quiet.

Mother left the window to sit in her overstuffed chair. "Third Sister, will you bring me some tea?"

148

"Mother, can I go out and play?" Fourth Sister asked.

Mother nodded absently. Second Brother followed Fourth Sister down the stairs.

Shao-shao was about to join them when Mother stretched out her arm. "Come sit with me, Shao-shao."

Shao-shao squeezed in beside her, resting his cheek on her cool silk shoulder, listening to her stories about Hangchow, when she and Father lived behind the bakery.

"I was so young then," she said, more to herself than him. "Younger than Third Sister. My father had been dead for three years. My mother told me I was lucky to have a father-in-law, and she was right. I didn't mind the hard work. We all worked so hard in those days. And how frugal we were! We saved every penny so Father could start his own business. Life was easier when we moved to Shanghai. Those were the good days, before the war. . . ." Her voice trailed off and she fell silent.

She looked down into the courtyard as if she could see beyond Second Brother and Tak-ming hitting Ping-Pong balls, beyond Mei-ling and Fourth Sister skipping rope, beyond the tree and open windows, beyond the rooftops, far away into her next life.

Now that summer vacation had come at last, everyone gathered in the courtyard to play. Everyone but Li-sha. She did not bring her little brother out anymore. Shao-shao did not see her again until the day the scrap collectors came to their neighborhood. He and Yun-lung were playing Ping-Pong on a makeshift table under the tree when noise from the street startled Shao-shao so that he fumbled Yun-lung's serve.

Metal clanged against metal, as if two swordsmen had stepped from the pages of *The Three Kingdoms* and were dueling in the alley. Shao-shao and Yun-lung looked at each other, put down their paddles, and warily crossed the courtyard.

Up the alley, a Chinese laborer, using a hammer and crowbar, pried wavy metal bars from the windows of a house. Two other Chinese laborers leaned against a cart. One held a sack heavy with mysterious objects. A Japanese soldier, armed with a pistol, shouted instructions.

Every blow of the hammer seemed to shake Shao-shao's bones. He looked at Yun-lung out of the corner of his eye. Yun-lung looked scared, too. They could never concentrate on Ping-Pong now, so they might as well stay and watch. Shao-shao could guess what was in the bag. The Japanese had been scouring the city for scrap metal to make weapons. They were taking things they hadn't bothered with earlier, like doorplates and pedicab wheels.

Up and down the alley, Chinese children and grown-ups leaned against house walls watching. Shao-shao wondered if they were as frightened as he was. Their faces revealed nothing.

When the laborers moved down the alley, Shao-shao and Yun-lung edged away from the safety of the

150

courtyard gate to follow them. They stood where they could see into Li-sha's backyard. She watched the scrap collectors from her back steps, gripping her little brother's hand. Her father stood behind them, touching Li-sha's shoulder.

The Chinese laborers continued down the block. Shao-shao and Yun-lung moved, too, keeping a safe distance. The laborers' backs glistened with sweat as they took turns hammering, pulling, and pushing the cart. By the time they reached the end of the block, the cart was so heavily loaded that two of them had to push it.

"They're heading back to Nanking Road," Yun-lung whispered.

"Do you think they'll come into our courtyard?" Shao-shao asked.

"I don't know," Yun-lung answered.

The hammer slammed against a metal window bar. Shao-shao jumped, as if the laborer had struck him in the ribs. But he stood by Yun-lung, trying not to shake, as the scrap collectors moved slowly toward them.

Mr. Chen spoke to the soldier in Japanese through the fancy iron gate. The soldier spat out a curt reply and shook his head. Mr. Chen said something more, but the soldier interrupted, waving him back to his steps. There Mr. Chen stood, flushed in the heat, as the soldiers broke the hinges of the lotus gate.

At the first blow, Li-sha shuddered and blinked. She lifted her little brother to her hip. He fussed and struggled, but she held him tightly, never taking her eyes from the laborers. They wrenched the gate off its hinges and beat the delicate iron grillwork with a hammer, bending and breaking it so it would fit into the cart.

Yun-lung plucked Shao-shao's elbow. "We'll be next," he whispered. They ran for home.

Shao-shao joined his family to watch the scrap collectors from the safety of the family room. For a moment, he thought Father stood behind him, as Li-sha's father had. Then he remembered Father was gone.

They began with the Shihs' house. Would they go inside?

Shao-shao gripped his elbows, trying to control his trembling. He thought of the woks in the kitchen, the cooking knives. Could the scrap collectors smash them as they smashed Li-sha's gate? Could they take the iron stove in the kitchen? If a Japanese soldier could come into the courtyard and take whatever he wanted, what would keep him from coming into the house?

Soon they might knock a crowbar against the bars of the downstairs windows.

Before they had finished at the Shihs' house, a truck rumbled slowly down the alley. The driver called to the soldier. The laborers gathered up their tools and pushed the cart, laden with sacks, toward the truck. The sound of its motor faded away toward the east, and the Japanese barracks on the edge of the French Sector.

"Will they come back tomorrow?" Shao-shao asked.

"Sooner or later, they'll be back," Gao-ma predicted.

"They must be really desperate for metal if they're taking window bars," Third Sister said.

"Why don't the pigs give up?" Gao-ma asked. "Why do they keep making us suffer?"

13. Air Raids
July 1945

EVERY MORNING, SHAO-SHAO WOKE EX-
pecting to hear a hammer striking metal. But when
the scrap collectors did not return after several
weeks, he almost forgot about them. Gao-ma fussed
about not having a grown man in the house, but
Shao-shao was glad to be free of Father's scolding,
free to do as he pleased in the courtyard and streets,
steaming with July heat.

He hunted crickets every night. Gao-ma never re-
fused to go with him. He stopped when eight large
cricket pots sat in a row along his wall. There was no
space for more. Second Brother said he couldn't sleep
with all the chirping, but Mother and Gao-ma only
laughed and said it would take more than cricket
songs to keep Second Brother from sleeping.

Fourth Sister was not so happy. A few weeks after
Father left, Gao-ma discovered she had head lice.
Mother blamed Gao-ma and Gao-ma blamed the
slovenly nurses of the girls at school, especially Mei-

ling's servant. But it did not really matter who was responsible because Fourth Sister was the one who suffered. Gao-ma cut Fourth Sister's hair short and shaved her head. After that she hardly ever went outside. Cousin Wei-fun came to play with her sometimes, but Mei-ling and her other friends from school left her entirely alone. They said she looked like a boy now, and they wouldn't play with boys.

When he was in the alley, Shao-shao sometimes saw Li-sha playing with her younger brother in her backyard. She tossed him his ball and shuttlecock, but she hardly ever smiled at him. Without the lotus gate, Li-sha's backyard looked forlorn and unprotected.

Shao-shao tried to think of something he could do to cheer Li-sha up. She wore barrettes all the time. Perhaps a new pair would make her happy. A cloth seller in the open-air market up Nanking Road sold pretty ones, but Japanese soldiers and civilians frequented the area, so he couldn't go alone. Of course he couldn't go with Yun-lung and Tai-shen, or Second Brother. He did not dare ask Mother or Third Sister to go with him; they would forbid him to give a present to Li-sha. That left Gao-ma.

She seemed willing to do almost anything he asked these days. Still, he didn't want to tell her beforehand what he planned. He would find out when she was going shopping there and ask to go along. As the weeks of July went by, every day or so he asked her until at last she said yes.

They joined the stream of pedestrians on the warm

sidewalks, skirting a knot of Japanese soldiers. Shao-shao waited while Gao-ma bargained in the small grocery that sold the best dried shrimp and cellophane noodles in the neighborhood. "I could buy this for two cents before the war," she scolded. "You jack up the price and call it 'inflation.'"

"What can I do?" The shopkeeper spread his hands helplessly.

Shao-shao helped Gao-ma select vegetables from a peasant's pushcart, then wandered past the candy man toward the cloth seller's cart.

Gao-ma stopped to greet the bookseller, sunning outside his shop. Whenever Shao-shao bought a kung-fu novel there, she told him about the time, soon after they had come back to Shanghai, when Japanese soldiers had stopped her in front of his bookstore for questioning. The bookseller knew some Japanese and had been brave enough to translate. "They might have arrested me if it hadn't been for him," Gao-ma always said. "He's an educated man with a kind heart."

Pretending to be idly curious, Shao-shao stood beside the cloth seller's cart, trying to figure out which barrettes Li-sha would like best.

Gao-ma came up behind him. "I'd bet my year's wages you want a present for Miss Chen Li-sha."

Shao-shao put his finger to his lips and looked anxiously around the square. Suppose someone heard her? He took a plain white pair, clipped to a cardboard backing, off the cart. "Do you think she'd like these?" he whispered to Gao-ma.

156

"Girls like things more fancy. Why don't you get her those?" She pointed to a pair of red barrettes in the shape of butterflies.

Shao-shao paid for the barrettes and put them in his pocket.

"Now let's go home," Gao-ma said. "It's nearly noon, and I'm ready for a rest."

Shao-shao could not give Li-sha the barrettes because the boys were playing in the courtyard that afternoon. Second Brother went off with his pellet gun for a while. Shao-shao was tossing coins with Yun-lung and Tak-ming when he returned. He held up a pair of limp sparrows. "Help me pluck them," he said.

"I'll get the water," Tak-ming offered.

When he brought a pot of boiling water from his kitchen, Second Brother dropped the small bodies in to soak. After a few minutes, he fished them out, and they all began to pluck.

"Do you think your servant would cook them for us?" Second Brother asked Tak-ming.

Tak-ming shook his head, laughing.

"Gao-ma wouldn't either," Second Brother said.

"We could build a fire here," Shao-shao suggested.

"Good idea!" Yun-lung jumped to his feet. "I'll get some sticks."

"We'll need a little wok," Second Brother said. "You ask Gao-ma, Shao-shao. She likes you better than me."

Shao-shao jumped up and ran home, caught in the excitement of this new game.

"Don't forget the soy sauce," Second Brother called after him.

The kitchen was empty. Gao-ma and Ah-fong must be cleaning upstairs. Shao-shao rummaged through the shelves and found a small wok, a wooden stirring paddle, bottles of soy sauce and oil. In the courtyard, a fire blazed in a ring of stones. The heat washed over Shao-shao's face. The smoke rose in the humid air, acrid on his nostrils.

Second Brother poured a little oil in the wok and set it over the fire. When it sizzled, he dropped the tiny naked birds in. They seemed much smaller without their feathers.

"Let me stir!" Shao-shao demanded, holding tight to the paddle when Second Brother tried to take it from him. He poked the birds and turned them over, then surrendered the paddle to Yun-lung. They took turns until the sparrows were done.

"You get the first bite," Tak-ming said to Second Brother.

Second Brother held the sparrow between the tips of his fingers and nibbled gingerly. He grimaced. "Boney, but good," he said. "You have the next bite, Yun-lung."

Yun-lung took the bird and looked at it for a long moment, then took a tiny bite off the leg. Just as he passed it to Shao-shao, Third Sister came through the courtyard gate, her face flushed, her dress stained with sweat.

"What are you doing?" she called. "Who said you could light a fire in the courtyard?" Shao-shao

158

couldn't remember ever seeing her so upset. "What are you eating?"

Before any of them could answer, she grabbed Shao-shao's shoulder and pulled him up. "Put out that fire right now!" She looked at the telltale pile of brown feathers. "What would Father say if he saw you eating sparrows?"

Shao-shao did not want to imagine what Father would say.

The sticks had burned. Second Brother and Tak-ming stomped the ashes and tossed the remaining sparrow on the cobblestones. The cats would find it, Shao-shao thought as Third Sister pulled him toward the house. Second Brother grabbed the wok and followed them.

"We'll have to throw away that wok," she exploded. "Sparrows!"

Mother called down from the family-room doorway, "You're home early. I thought Yuan-yi had the whole afternoon off."

Third Sister's friend Yuan-yi had been working at the Metropole Hotel since the end of the term at St. John's. When she had the afternoon off, she and Third Sister usually went shopping or to the movies.

Shao-shao twisted away when Third Sister stopped for breath on the landing. Behind them, Second Brother slipped into the kitchen with the wok and the soy sauce bottle. If Mother didn't see the evidence, she probably wouldn't scold them. As she herself said, "What the eye doesn't see, the heart doesn't worry about."

159

"Some Japanese soldiers started following us. They wouldn't leave us alone." Third Sister—calm, reasonable Third Sister—sounded as if she might cry.

Mother came quickly downstairs and took her arm. The turn of her mouth and the look in her eye told Shao-shao she was shocked, but her voice betrayed no emotion. "Come and sit down," she said. "Tell me what happened."

"The things they said!" Third Sister sank into the chair. "We pretended not to understand Japanese, so they switched to Chinese. They kept following us. Finally we jumped on a moving streetcar and lost them."

"Shao-shao, go and ask Ah-fong to make some tea," Mother said. She stroked Third Sister's arm, saying, "Try to forget it. Be thankful they did you no harm."

In the kitchen, Shao-shao spotted the wok, hastily jammed in a shelf where it did not belong. Second Brother had wiped it, but it was still oily and streaked with soy sauce.

Ah-fong came in through the back-stairs door just as Shao-shao put the wok in its proper place.

"A clear night," she observed as she poured water into a teacup. "Perfect weather for an air raid."

By the time Third Sister had finished her tea and calmed down, Fourth Sister came home from Grandmother's house, where she had been playing with Cousin Wei-fun. The servants laid out supper dishes,

160

and Third Sister never did tell Mother about the cooked sparrows.

After supper, Shao-shao took a few grains of rice upstairs to feed his crickets. He knelt by the clay jars and carefully slid back a cover. He did not want this cricket to escape, even though it was his smallest and a sure loser, for it was the one he had caught at Li-sha's.

An air-raid siren sounded, sudden, insistent. The cricket jumped out of the pot.

Shao-shao tried to catch it, but it slipped through his fingers. Downstairs, Mother called his name. Footsteps pounded on the stairs: Fourth Sister ran into the girls' bedroom to turn off a light she had left burning. "Hurry!" she cried. "Turn out the lights. Come down."

Shao-shao peered under his desk, lifted the carpet. He could not find the cricket. When Third Sister called him from the landing, he gave up and turned out his light.

In the family room, Mother asked, "Is everything dark upstairs?" She told Shao-shao to pull down the shades, her voice brittle, uncertain.

As he pulled down a black-out shade, Shao-shao thought of the man Father had hidden in the storage room. Was he somewhere in the city, flashing secret signals to help American fliers find their targets?

Searchlight beams moved across the sky. The Japanese were trying to spot the bombers so antiaircraft guns could shoot them down.

Around the courtyard, he could still see lights in the neighboring houses. Not in the Chens'. Pulling down another shade, he remembered how Li-sha smiled in spite of herself when she'd brushed his crickets with a frayed stem of grass. Tomorrow he would give her the barrettes.

As he reached for the last shade, he heard staccato voices hammering out Japanese. He was so scared he nearly let the shade roll back up. Trembling, he leaned against the wall and peered past the shade into the courtyard.

Mother was covering the last lamp with its black-out shade.

"Soldiers are coming into the courtyard." Shao-shao could keep his voice low, but he could not keep it from quavering. Against the eerie glow of search-lights he saw black shapes gather near the courtyard entrance, bayonets bobbing as they moved. He pulled away from the window and closed his eyes, rubbing his open, sweaty palms against his pants, blood pounding in his ears.

"They're knocking at the Chows' house," Second Brother reported.

"Get away from that window," Gao-ma hissed.

"They'll come to every house." Mother's voice, no longer a whisper, rang out like a scream. In its frame of smooth black hair, her face looked chalky, her eyes strangely bright.

She stared at Shao-shao as if she had never seen him before and turned quickly back toward her bed-room. The family stood frozen, Shao-shao and Second Brother against the wall, the sisters beside the table, Gao-ma supporting herself on the back of the chair, Ah-fong pressed against the back-stairs door, ready to bolt downstairs at any moment. In the silence, Shao-shao heard the rustle of sheets, the muffled grunt of mattress springs.

Outside, a door slammed. Heavy feet tramped against the cobblestones. A fist pounded against a door and harsh Japanese commands rang out.

Mother shuffled out of the darkness, swaying on her small feet, holding a folded paper. Shao-shao stared at the paper, wondering what it was.

"I've got to hide this," she muttered, "or they'll find it."

She lifted up a chair cushion. "If they see it, they'll know where he was born."

She dropped the cushion, looked desperately around the room, opened a chest.

"It can't be too obvious. My mattress is the first place they'd look."

She closed the chest, still holding the paper. "They can have our gold bars. What is more precious than my son?"

Mother knelt beside the rug and lifted up a corner. Suddenly Shao-shao understood. The folded paper was his birth certificate, proof that he was a British subject. The soldiers could arrest him.

He could hear the Japanese soldiers knocking at the Wus' next door.

She let the rug corner go and met his eyes. Her rapid, erratic movements had loosened some hair from her bun and it fell across her cheek. "They'll take him away," she moaned. "They'll kill him with forced labor, like they're killing his First Brother. Oldest and youngest . . ."

Mother rose and staggered to the table, gripping a chair as Gao-ma rushed to support her. The birth certificate shook in her hand. "Where can I hide it?" she asked, looking at her children. Third Sister pointed and whispered, "Up there." Fourth Sister pulled out a chair and helped Mother up so she could reach the top of the high, carved chest.

Would he have time to hide? His heart pounding so hard it seemed to shake his whole body, Shao-shao looked out. Against the searchlight beams ranging the night sky, he saw the silhouette of soldiers' caps, the glint of moving bayonets.

Then the pounding echoed up the stairs, almost shaking the house. The soldiers were at their door.

"I'll go, Mother." Third Sister took two firm steps toward the stairs, her braid swinging over her shoulder, her cheeks fiery red against her white skin.

Mother slipped down from the chair and grabbed Third Sister's arm. "You stay here. You've seen enough of Japanese soldiers today. Gao-ma and I will go."

With Gao-ma behind her, she left the room as quickly as she could. They could hear her light, labored steps on the stairs, the creak of the door, Chinese words spit out in a thick Japanese accent.

"Lights on. Bad, bad. We come in see."

164

Booted feet thumped upstairs. Three Japanese soldiers burst into the family room, small dark men in brown uniforms, carrying their bayonets before them, sharp enough to pierce a belly. For a long moment, Shao-shao looked straight into their faces. One was older than the others, his skin etched with lines like Grandmother's. There was a wart on his jaw, and his mouth curled in a snarl, like a dog's. Horrified, Shao-shao dropped his eyes to stare at six dirty boots. Suddenly, he felt an intense longing to see Father, solid and commanding in his Western clothes, standing there in the family room, talking to the soldiers. Father could make them go away.

Third Sister said something calmly in Japanese. The older one replied contemptuously, like a teacher reproving a foolish student. Third Sister turned to Ah-fong, who stared at the floor, wide-eyed and pale. "There is a light on in the kitchen," she said. Go down and turn it out." Ah-fong scuttled down the back stairs like a scared rabbit.

Shao-shao resisted the urge to glance at the top of the carved chest. The chair Mother had used stood beside it. Would they search the room? Would they find his birth certificate? He forced himself to keep his eyes down, remembering Mother's favorite proverb. If he didn't meet their eyes, they might ignore him. He could not fight them. All he could do was try to avoid notice.

"Next time we arrest," the eldest soldier warned, then barked a command in Japanese. The soldiers turned and pounded downstairs, leaving the odor of sweat and gunpowder behind them. Shao-shao heard the front door slam.

No one moved.

He heard the soldiers leave the courtyard.

Mother collapsed into the chair beside the table, panting, her delicate hands clasping and unclasping in the circle of muted lamplight. "If only Father had been here," she said softly, then dropped her face into her hands. Slowly, silently, each of the children came to sit around the table. No one said anything. No one picked up the newspapers or kung-fu novels piled on the table. They sat waiting, listening to the distant rumble of bombs. Mother whispered something so low and broken that Shao-shao did not recognize at first the familiar verses of her favorite prayer.

When the "all clear" sounded, Mother raised her head. She had not been crying, but there were red marks where she had pressed her fingers against her forehead. "Gao-ma," she said, her voice thick and rusty as if she had not used it for a long time, "Shao-shao and Fourth Sister should be in bed."

Later when Second Brother came to bed, Shao-shao lay awake, still listening to his crickets sing, wondering where the lost one was. Gao-ma had not let him search for it.

He could not stop the fear shuddering through his stomach and throat.

In the middle of the night, Mother came in and found Shao-shao still awake. She sat on his bed and stroked his hair. "The harbor is in flames," she said. "Everyone in Shanghai can see. The Americans must have hit an oil tank. The Japs are losing, Shao-shao. Someday they'll be gone."

As the crickets sang in the dark, Mother sat with him, humming an old lullaby, until he fell asleep.

14. Blue Sky, White Sun
August 1945

THICK CLOUDS HUNG LOW AFTER THE rainstorm, bringing an early dusk. Shao-shao stared into lighted windows across the courtyard as a two-note chorus of crickets throbbed in the still air. He could see only indistinct shadows through the Chens' closed shades. At Yun-lung's house, the Chows gathered around their table for supper.

We'll all be left in peace tonight, he thought. It's too cloudy for an air raid.

He touched the barrettes at the bottom of his pocket. The card that held them was battered now, after ten days in his drawer. He had tried to deliver them several times, but each time he had lost his nerve. Li-sha could leave any day now. Tonight he must give them to her.

He had finished supper quickly and left everyone else at the table behind him, listening to news from Chungking. Now he stood by the window, waiting for the right moment to leave. He couldn't go whenever he wanted, because guests were at the table.

First Sister and Brother Ma had come for supper, bringing pork and vegetables from the Ma family farm outside the city. "Uncle gave us plenty, so you enjoy it," Brother Ma had said as he presented the food to Mother.

"Please, no turnips tonight!" Shao-shao said, when he saw what Brother Ma had brought. Everyone he knew was sick of turnips.

Fat Ming had come with food only once since Father left, and they had not had pork in several weeks. Remembering Father was like flying a kite in a strong wind. You could not see the kite, but you could feel it pulling so hard you nearly left the ground.

Fourth Sister, sitting close to First Sister, had almost finished her third bowl of rice. This summer she was always hungry. All her clothes were too small, and Mother had no money to buy new ones. So Fourth Sister and Shao-shao shared Second Brother's outgrown shirts and pants. Brother Ma swept his hand over her stubble of hair and called her "Little Brother." Shao-shao knew she didn't like that. But what could they do about Brother Ma's teasing?

While the announcer described another American attack on Japan, Second Brother made noises like exploding bombs. "Tokyo's flattened," he sang out.

"If they're blockaded, how long can they hold out?" Mother asked. "They're running out of food in Tokyo."

"All the Japs will starve to death!" Second Brother chanted.

Shao-shao shut out their voices and listened to the insistent song of the crickets. His cricket had sung its own victory song that afternoon as it spread its fangs and chased Tak-ming's around the pot.

When the Chungking station faded out, Mother turned off the radio and filled teacups around the table.

"Any news from Father?" First Sister asked softly, as if she was afraid a stranger would overhear.

"Fat Ming says he's got a government post. The salary's small, but it comes with a house. We might be able to join him soon."

"Oh, Mother, do you have to go at all?" First Sister put down her chopsticks and leaned toward Mother. "The war could be over in a few months."

"There's something else I couldn't tell you over the telephone," Mother said. Her voice dropped so low that Shao-shao strained to hear her.

"Your father is on their list. There's a Japanese officer at the train station waiting to arrest him if he comes back to Shanghai."

Shao-shao stared at the tree next to the Wangs' house. Tangled in its rain-wet branches was the skeleton of a kite the Shih boys had flown in the courtyard before they left. No one could reach it, so it had hung there all summer, lost and alone.

For the last ten days he had faced Japanese soldiers in waking and sleeping nightmares. He had never imagined that Father might not come back.

170

He dreamed he heard the clash of metal on Li-sha's gate. But her father was with her. Sometimes he woke terrified that Mother was lost and he could not find her, that only Gao-ma stood between him and the bayonets. Sometimes he woke sick with guilt, as if he had sent Father away with his angry thoughts.

He needed to breathe the rain-damp air and hear the sound of crickets. Now. He turned and spoke, interrupting First Sister. "Yun-lung's got a new cricket. Can I go and see?"

"Yes, if you're back before dark," Mother answered.

"Watch out for falling bombs," Brother Ma teased.

Li-sha was not long in coming to her empty gateway. "First Brother didn't take a nap," she said. "So he went to sleep early. I saw you and Tak-ming have a cricket fight today. Who won?"

"Mine did. He's won every fight so far. If he keeps it up, he'll be champion of the whole neighborhood."

"Is he the one you caught in my yard?"

"No, that one escaped the night—" He almost said, "—the night of the big air raid," but he stopped in time. He didn't want to mention the air raid to her. "He escaped," he finished lamely.

"I'm sorry. Where is he now?"

"I think he went back outside. He sang in my room for a while. Then he stopped."

Shao-shao stopped, too. He couldn't get up his nerve to give her the barrettes. Li-sha said nothing more, so they stood silently as dusk filled the street.

At last Shao-shao blurted out: "I was afraid you'd leave before I could give these to you." He pulled the barrettes out of his pocket. The card was battered around the edges, but the red butterflies looked bright and new.

She stared at them for a long moment, then at him. "Thank you, Shao-shao."

She smiled.

"Do you like them?"

"Oh, yes. They're very pretty."

"Good. I was afraid you wouldn't."

"I don't have any butterflies. My nurse only buys me plain ones." She smoothed back her hair, touching the black metal barrettes she wore. She looked at him, turning her head to one side. "Shao-shao, if I go away, would you remember me?"

Shao-shao hesitated, embarrassed. "Maybe you won't go away," he stammered. "Maybe your father will—will change jobs."

"That's what Papa said. But Mama said we'll have to leave."

"Then we could write each other."

Li-sha put the red butterflies carefully in her pocket. "I'd like that," she said.

Every day Shao-shao's big cricket fought and won, until it had beaten all the crickets in the neighborhood. Pei-fu, a classmate who lived eight blocks away, also owned an unbeaten champion. A showdown was inevitable.

A match was arranged, to be held in Shao-shao's

courtyard. All their friends came to see. Everyone cheered as the crickets sprang at each other. They grappled, parted, and came back for more. Neither would give up.

Shao-shao imagined his cricket was a famous warrior, like the ones in the operas. The music that filled the courtyard the moment his cricket lunged seemed part of this fantasy.

That lunge finished the fight. Pei-fu's cricket knew he was beaten. He turned tail and crawled up the side of the pot, trembling. Shao-shao cheered. Yun-lung and Tai-shen pounded him on the shoulders, while the stirring Chinese melody played by a Western orchestra poured out of the second-floor windows. A victory song for his cricket.

Grown-ups—Mother, Yun-lung's servant, Mrs. Wu—shouted across the courtyard.

"Do you hear?"

"Can it be true?"

"What does it mean?"

Only the Chens' house stood silent. Its shutters had been closed in the suffocating August heat since America's new bomb destroyed two Japanese cities, Hiroshima and Nagasaki. Chungking radio called it an "atom bomb." Gao-ma said it was divine retribution.

Shao-shao knew the Chens had not left because Li-sha's nurse went out early to shop for food. She walked with her head bent, her shoulders hunched, as if she wished she were invisible.

"It's not from Chungking," Mrs. Wu yelled. "It's a Shanghai station."

Why was she so excited? Of course it had to be the Shanghai station. Chungking Radio never came in at this time of day, and it was never this clear.

"They've given up!" Yun-lung's servant yelled.

"Come in! Come in right now!" Mother called. Shao-shao grabbed his cricket pot and reluctantly followed Second Brother upstairs. In the family room, Fourth Sister and Cousin Wei-fun were cutting out paper dolls. "Do you hear that?" Mother told them. "We must listen. There's sure to be an announcement after."

The children stared at each other, shaking their heads in puzzlement. Mother smiled broadly at Gao-ma.

"They don't remember. They're too young." She swung her head in rhythm with the music. "It's our national anthem," she told him. "The Japs would never allow it before."

The anthem broke off in the middle of its fifth repetition. Opera music followed, but no announcement was made.

Late in the afternoon, Third Sister burst into the family room, her eyes bright with excitement. "The Chinese flag was flying over the Cathay Hotel! You could see it a block away!"

"Why won't they surrender? Don't the turnip-heads know they're beaten?" Second Brother asked.

"They're worried about the Emperor. They don't want the Americans to humiliate him," Third Sister answered.

174

Mother looked out the window, into the brilliant blue sky. "Who would have imagined such a bomb?"

"What will Father do now?" Third Sister asked.

"I don't know. I wish he could come home."

"He can, now, can't he?" Shao-shao asked. "If we've won?" Suddenly, he wanted to see Father walking across the courtyard.

Mother shook her head wearily. "They're still fighting out there." She swept her open hand, seeming to include all the countryside between Chungking and Shanghai. "As soon as the Japs leave, we'll have the Communist rebels to worry about."

"And the Japs are still in charge here." Third Sister fell into a chair.

"I hope Father has enough money for bribes," Mother said, staring into space.

An image of Father in Chinese clothes, passing tanks, picking his way around land mines, with bombs exploding around him came suddenly into Shao-shao's mind. He ran to Mother and put his head on her lap, like a baby.

A day passed. Then another. And another. Still no news. Shao-shao, Yun-lung, and Tai-shen spent their afternoons wandering along Nanking Road. People filled the sidewalks, shopping, gossiping, ignoring the Japanese soldiers slouching against the store fronts. There were no more roadblocks. No one saw the soldiers practicing defense drills. They were waiting, like everyone else.

A week after the American bomb set Hiroshima on fire, the evening radio announced: "The Japanese have surrendered."

Who could believe it? Who would govern Shanghai now?

The next morning Shao-shao, Yun-lung, and Tai-shen went to see what was happening on Nanking Road. They pushed through the crowds as far as the open-air market where Shao-shao had bought Li-sha's barrettes. The bookseller sat in front of his store as usual, and pushcarts selling candy, fruit, vegetables, dumplings, cookware, and cloth stood in their usual places.

Three Japanese soldiers loitered by the fruit seller's cart. Shao-shao ventured a quick glance at them. They wore no ammunition belts and swung their rifles carelessly as they chatted in Japanese with an old civilian.

"Let's look at kung-fu books," Tai-shen said. He had taken two steps into the bookstore when the air above resounded with the crackle of static.

The boys stood still, looking for a loudspeaker.

The soldiers broke off their conversation in mid-sentence.

Up and down the street, the sounds of bargaining and conversation faded away. Three pedicab drivers stopped in their tracks. All faces, Chinese and Japanese, turned toward the dark metal horn hanging under the eaves of the apothecary shop.

Suddenly, a voice boomed out of the horn, a seri-

176

ous voice, speaking Japanese, but distorted, as if coming from far away.

Japanese soldiers sprang to attention. The voice stopped. The street was so quiet Shao-shao could hear the old bookseller draw in an amazed breath. Then another voice spoke, a low voice, echoing, the syllables drawn out. It sounded like a chant or a prayer.

The old man with the soldiers stared at the loudspeaker, open-mouthed, then slowly dropped to his knees and touched his head to the dusty sidewalk.

Shao-shao stared boldly at the nearest soldier and realized that he saw nothing, nobody. He raised his chin and tightened his mouth. His eyes, fixed on the loudspeaker, were puzzled.

Shao-shao stared and stared at the soldier, while the voice from the loudspeaker continued its rhythmic chant. How young he was! He couldn't be much older than Second Brother.

Beside them, the bookseller let out a deep breath.

"Who's that?" The candy man asked. "Is it . . . ?"

"The Emperor Hirohito," the bookseller whispered, pointing his chin to the loudspeaker. "I can hardly understand him. But he's accepted America's terms."

"He's giving up?" the candy man whispered, astonished.

"He says he doesn't want his subjects to suffer anymore," the bookseller whispered.

"We're free?"

The bookseller nodded.

Shao-shao understood how the candy man felt. He could not believe it either, could not understand how the Emperor, so proud on his white horse, would admit defeat.

When the voice from the loudspeaker stopped, the crowd stood stunned. The young soldier near Shao-shao trembled, biting his lip as tears slid down his cheeks. He gripped his rifle, but Shao-shao felt afraid no longer. The soldier's power was gone. His Emperor had given up.

Then all around them, like bells pealing from the French Church, Chinese voices rose: "China Ten Thousand Years!" and "Generalissimo Chiang Ten Thousand Years!" Soon everyone was cheering and shouting and laughing, surging from the sidewalks to the street. The soldiers slipped away down an alley and disappeared. Pedicab drivers mounted their bicycles, but they could not go forward because of the crowd. Two young Chinese women jumped from their pedicab, laughing. One handed the driver a handful of bills, and they joined the crowd on Nanking Road.

The candy man tossed each boy a lollipop. "Now all our troubles are over!" he cried. "Celebrate!"

Shao-shao stood in front of the bookstore, the lollipop sweet on his tongue. His excitement quickened as waves of people surged by, each group more joyful than the last.

Not everyone was noisy with glee. An old woman in patched cotton stood silently on the sidewalk, her eyes closed, her fingers counting prayer beads, her lips forming the words of a sutra. The old man with her raised his eyes skyward, unmoved by the singing children skipping around them.

The boys headed up the street, sucking their lollipops. A bang like a gunshot sent Shao-shao diving for cover.

Yun-lung grabbed his arm, laughing. "That's a firecracker, dummy," he shouted.

Shao-shao leaned against Yun-lung, laughing, giddy with relief. Tai-shen grabbed Yun-lung's other arm and pulled them along, and so they danced up Nanking Road, shouting "China Ten Thousand Years! China Ten Thousand Years!"

Outside a stationery shop, a man held a fistful of tiny paper flags. They were bright red, with a sky-blue rectangle in the corner. On this piece of blue sky shone a white sun.

"Chinese flags, only a penny!" he called. The boys each bought one and waved them over their heads as they ran toward the alley that led to their courtyard.

They slowed down when they saw two soldiers walking ahead of them. The soldiers hunched over, ducking their heads as if they hoped no one would see them. The crowd left a space around them.

A rotten turnip struck the younger soldier in the shoulder. Shao-shao heard it thud. As the people around him jeered, Shao-shao crouched against a wall, fear swelling in his throat.

The young soldier spun around, pointing his rifle toward the crowd. A tomato caught him as he turned, splatting across his chest. He cursed, ready to shoot, his finger on the trigger.

There was nowhere Shao-shao could hide.

Quickly, the other soldier shouted a command. He pushed the gun barrel toward the street, so the bayonet tip crashed against the cobblestones.

"Go home, rotten turnips!" someone yelled in Chinese.

The older soldier stared at the crowd, his eyes wide. Shao-shao recognized his lined face, the wart on his mouth. He had come to their house the night of the air raid. Now he looked as ragged as a used firecracker shell. He couldn't scare Shao-shao anymore.

The pair turned, wearily shouldered their rifles, bowed their heads, and continued down the alley. They did not look back to see who threw the turnip that landed at their heels.

In the courtyard the boys found a celebration more festive than any New Year's Eve they had ever known. Chinese flags hung from the Wus' window. Servants had left their work to gather under the tree, joking and laughing together. Even shy Ah-fong blushed and smiled at the Wangs' old houseboy. Wu Mei-ling linked arms with Fourth Sister as if she had never said she would not be friends.

Pei-fu, Second Brother, and Tak-ming greeted Shao-shao and his friends with raucous shouts: "Did you hear? We've won! The Japs surrendered!"

"Who painted the *V*?" Shao-shao looked up at

the English letter painted on the wall below the family-room window.

"I did!" Second Brother shouted, holding up his two fingers to make the V for Victory sign.

"Hey! No more Kamakura!" Tak-ming cried, and the Middle School boys waved their fists and cheered the defeat of their hated Japanese teacher.

The windows of every house in the courtyard were flung wide open. Every house but the Chens'. Was Li-sha in her room, peeping around a drawn shade, watching them?

"No more Stringbean Kamakura!" Second Brother shouted.

"No more dirty Kamakura!" Pei-fu took up the cry, even though he was in Elementary School and had never taken Japanese.

"No more dirty turnip-head Kamakura!" Tak-ming jumped up and down, shaking his fists. When the boys had exhausted their supply of insults, Pei-fu pointed to the Chens' front door. "There's a Chinese Jap!" he shouted. "Are you happy today, Mr. Chen?"

"Filthy traitor, filthy traitor," the boys cried at the Chens' closed windows, jumping up and down in rhythm with their taunts. Fourth Sister and Mei-ling added their voices to the chant.

Tak-ming ran into his house.

Shao-shao pulled at Yun-lung's arm. "Let's go to the field and see what's happening," he said, but Yun-lung paid no attention.

Tak-ming returned with an armful of turnips. The older boys grabbed them eagerly and flung them at the Chens' house. Tak-ming opened his arms and let the rest of the turnips fall to the cobblestones. Tai-shen, Yun-lung, and the girls scrambled for them.

"Here you are, Shao-shao," said Yun-lung, tossing a turnip. Shao-shao caught it.

The turnips made a noise like distant antiaircraft guns as they struck the walls and shutters of the house. Shao-shao's turnip thudded against the collaborator's front door.

Second Brother pulled a handful of mud balls from his pocket. He hurled one at the Chens' steps, yelling "Bombs away!"

The explosion resounded against the courtyard walls.

"Direct hit!" Tak-ming yelled.

Pei-fu produced more mud balls. "Who wants one?" he asked.

Shao-shao looked up at the Chens' second-floor windows. Could Li-sha be watching through the shutters? The boys around him grabbed mud balls. He reached out to take one.

Mud balls blasted like small bombs against the Chens' house. The servants at the back of the courtyard laughed and cheered.

Tak-ming reached down for a last turnip. He aimed for the Chens' window.

When glass hit cobblestone, Shao-shao turned and ran for his door. It opened unexpectedly before him, and he tripped and fell against Mother.

"Li-sha was my friend." He fought back a sob.

She put her arms around him and touched her

cheek against his hair. She wiped tears from his face with her palm, whispering, "I know." Then she released him and turned him toward the stairs.

He stood on the landing by the storage room, wondering if Li-sha had seen him throw turnips and mud balls at her house.

In the vestibule, Mother called through the door to his brother and sister. "Stop that!" she cried. "Come inside this instant! You sound like a bunch of beggar children."

"Shao-shao," Third Sister called from the family room. "Come up and tell me what happened on Nanking Road." He ran upstairs to tell her about hearing the Emperor and getting free candy. Before he got to the part about the old soldier who had entered their house, Mother came in and leaned out the window to call Second Brother and Fourth Sister in once more.

"Sit down, Mother. I'll go get them," Third Sister said.

Mother collapsed on the sofa. "I don't know how your father will get back," she said. "Everyone in Chungking will be fighting for passes. I can't manage much longer, I can't. . . ."

She leaned her head back and closed her eyes, whispering an invocation to Buddha and her ancestors. "Please bring back my husband and my eldest son," she prayed.

Shao-shao knew she could not really celebrate until Father came home. He pictured Father, angry and strong, in control.

Yet he could not banish another picture from his mind, a picture of Li-sha standing inside her window and watching them throw turnips and mud balls at her house.

15. A Cup of Tea
August 1945

WILD DREAMS TROUBLED SHAO-SHAO'S sleep. Father and First Brother held guns with bayonets pointed at Li-sha. Shao-shao took her hand and pulled her into the street, but they ran into Japanese soldiers firing a machine gun. He woke with a start, his heart pounding, hearing the pop of firecrackers from Nanking Road.

Early light shone through the windows. Second Brother snored softly as Shao-shao dressed and put a handful of marbles in his pocket. Downstairs, he found Gao-ma in the kitchen, making the morning porridge.

"You're up early."

"Firecrackers woke me up. I couldn't go back to sleep, so I thought I'd go out while it was still cool."

"Don't go up to Nanking Road. The city's gone crazy."

"I won't. I promise." That promise would be easy to keep. The sounds of gaiety he heard last night had been mixed with more sinister noises: windows breaking, drunken singing. He did not have to tell Gao-ma where he meant to go.

His feet dragged as he turned out of the courtyard toward Li-sha's house. What would she say to him? But he couldn't stop. He had to see her. He squatted just inside her empty gateway and practiced shooting marbles.

It seemed like half an hour before he heard her light footsteps cross the garden. He jumped up to greet her. She looked awful. Her face was puffy; her eyes were red; her hair, usually so smooth and neat, seemed not to have been combed in days. The red butterfly barrettes were jammed in, holding back wisps that had slipped out of her braid.

But her mouth and eyes relaxed into the beginning of a smile. Perhaps she had not seen him throw that mud ball.

"No one else is awake," she whispered. "We stayed up most of the night, packing to leave. My nurse hardly helped at all. She doesn't want to go with us, but she has to, because no one else will take her."

Shao-shao stammered, "When are you leaving?"

"Tomorrow or the next day."

So soon, Shao-shao thought to himself. Was it because of what they had done yesterday? Why hadn't he stopped them? But how could he have stopped them? He had joined them himself.

Things were all mixed up. Every day Mother and Gao-ma wished the collaborators would leave. But he wanted Li-sha to stay.

186

"Where will you go?"

"To Canton, where we have cousins. We can't go to Harbin now. Papa says the Russians will be there, and we must go someplace where no one knows us."

"Maybe you'll come back."

"I don't think we'll ever come back." She tried to hold back a sob.

Before he thought, Shao-shao flung an arm around her shoulder. He felt her bones shaking under the thin fabric of her dress. After a bit, she stopped crying, and he dropped his arm but stood close to her.

"How about your birds?" he asked. "Can you take them with you?"

"Papa says no. I have to let them go."

"No, you mustn't! Can't you give them to someone?"

"No one speaks to me. I don't know anyone who will take them."

"I will."

"But your father—"

"He's not here," he interrupted. He didn't think it would matter if she knew. "I'll find them a good home before he gets back. If I can't, I'll take them to the pet store. Someone's sure to buy them."

She looked at him uncertainly, wiping her wet cheeks with her fingers. "Shall I . . ." she glanced back at her house.

He knew she'd want some time to say good-bye to them. "Your nurse could bring them to Gao-ma this evening. Mother won't mind. I'll tell Gao-ma right now."

"Thank you, Shao-shao." She pushed back her hair, letting her fingers rest lightly on the barrette. "I'll tell them not to be afraid. I'll tell them you're their friend."

Mother told Gao-ma to place the bird cage on a table in the family room. She pursed her lips and made noises to get the birds' attention. "They're pretty," she said. "I'll ask Grandmother's neighbor if he wants them."

"Jap birds!" Second Brother hooted.

"Li Chung, be quiet!" Mother spoke so sharply that Second Brother went back to his kung-fu novel and said nothing more.

The next morning when Shao-shao went down to feed the birds, he saw Mother and Third Sister standing by the window, looking out. "Shao-shao," Third Sister called softly. "The Chens are leaving."

Mother let Shao-shao slide in front of her. Mr. Chen walked ahead of his family, weighted down with suitcases. Mrs. Chen followed, carrying a suitcase in one hand and the baby on her hip. The nurse came last, a cloth bundle hanging from her shoulder. She held the little boy by one hand and Li-sha by the other. Li-sha dragged a suitcase that looked too heavy for her. A doll dangled from under her arm.

The servant stopped for a moment to speak to the boy. Li-sha looked up at Shao-shao's window, directly into his eyes.

Shao-shao waved.

If she saw him, she gave no sign. She stood there

until her nurse pulled her forward with an impatient jerk.

Mother put her hands on his shoulders, and they stood watching until the Chens left the courtyard.

First Sister telephoned every day for news of Father. At last, a telegram came from Chungking: "Return pass granted. Home soon." After that, Mother dressed in silk and wore makeup and her best jewelry.

Shao-shao liked to put his finger between the bars of the cage to stroke the bright feathers of Li-sha's birds. He knew they had to leave before Father got home. He didn't really mind, not when Mother was so worried about Father.

Shao-shao was surprised at how relieved he felt when Grandmother's elderly neighbor consented to take Li-sha's birds. "He'll be happy when he sees them," Gao-ma said. "He could never afford such beautiful birds." Mother, Third Sister, Shao-shao, and the birds rode to Grandmother's house in a pedicab. Third Sister went with Shao-shao to deliver the birds, and repeated everything he said about feeding and airing. The old man smiled and pinched Shao-shao's cheek as he thanked him for the pretty birds.

Meanwhile, the Americans arrived.

Before they came, they sent gifts. American bombers swept over the city, dropping parachutes that floated packages gently to earth. They aimed their packages at the Chapei District, north of the city, where Western prisoners stayed in camps. Often the parachutes landed somewhere else. Then the Chinese who found them would open the boxes and fight over their contents: canned meat, chocolate bars, cigarettes, chewing gum.

"Now remember, it's not for sucking; you never swallow it. Just chew," Tai-shen instructed Yun-lung and Shao-shao as he slipped off the green paper sleeve, unwrapped the silver foil, and broke the thin gray strip of gum in two. His father had been nearby when an American parachute came down, and now Tai-shen had two packages of chewing gum.

Shao-shao chewed cautiously. It had a strange taste, not very sweet, but interesting. And it was American.

Then a few American soldiers landed at the airport. The newspapers had a picture of the car that took them to the Metropole Hotel, where Third Sister's friend Kuo Yuan-yi worked.

"They're arranging transport for American prisoners of war," Mother told Gao-ma as they stood over the dinner table, staring at the papers. Close beside Mother, Shao-shao bent over the blurred picture of a dark car passing through streets jammed with Chinese. He could not see inside the car.

"I wish I could see them," he said.

"The whole city wants to see them," Mother replied. "But how do we know where they are?"

"I'm going to call Yuan-yi," Third Sister said. "She's sure to know."

Yuan-yi reported that the Americans were tall, full of jokes and laughter. Their enormous appetites threw the kitchen into complete confusion. They liked thick beefsteaks best, and they ate them almost raw. The hotel was swarming with White Russian and Chinese girls, all wanting a date with the Americans. She had heard that more Americans were coming, but she didn't know when.

Shao-shao thought about Li-sha every day, wondering where she was and what she was doing. He wished he could tell her that Grandmother's neighbor doted on her birds.

Soon another group of American soldiers drove into Shanghai, but they were inside the Metropole before Yuan-yi knew they had arrived.

Each afternoon, First Sister called. "Has Father telegrammed?" she asked.

Mother always answered, "No, not today."

Shao-shao was still angry with Father about the bird. He thought he always would be. But now he wanted Father back. The family was incomplete without Father at its head.

One morning toward the end of August, everyone was playing in the courtyard when two low-flying planes roared overhead.

Marbles scattered and a Ping-Pong ball bounced aimlessly. They all looked up. Shao-shao covered his ears, but the others waved frantically. As the planes departed, rising toward the west, grown-ups leaned out the windows. The boys yelled up at them.

"American!"

"Four engines!"

"Flying Fortress!"

"One-engine fighter!"

"Heading for the airport!"

"Why so low?" Mrs. Wang asked.

No one could answer that question.

At lunch Yuan-yi called to say a letter addressed to the manager of the Metropole Hotel had dropped from the four-engine Flying Fortress. The plane carried American newspaper writers, and they wanted a car from the Metropole to meet them at the airport.

"They'll have to drive along Nanking Road near the Racecourse," Third Sister said, as she put down the telephone. "Who wants to go see them?"

"I do! I do!" Shao-shao and Fourth Sister screamed, and Mother put her hands over her ears, laughing and complaining that they made more noise than the airplanes.

In a little over an hour, all the neighborhood children were standing with Third Sister along the curb beside Nanking Road near the corner of Kiangse. The crowd was thick already, and people selling paper flags had to push their way through it. Third Sister bought everyone an American flag and a Chinese flag. Shao-shao held them side by side. Instead of a white sun in its blue corner, the American flag had rows of stars. Where the Chinese flag was solid red, the American flag had red-and-white stripes. The Americans sometimes called their flag the Stars and Stripes, Teacher Bao told them.

Hours passed, and still the Americans did not come. Second Brother and Tak-ming ran down Kiangse Road to the Metropole, where the doorman told them the Japanese were holding the Americans at the airport.

"They *can't* take them prisoner," Third Sister gasped.

"No, never," a woman standing beside them said.

"The doorman says they're on their way." Second Brother bounced on his toes impatiently. The people around him repeated his words, and Shao-shao heard, "They're on their way, they're on their way," spreading like ripples from a pebble dropped in a pool.

To pass the time, Third Sister taught the children some English words. *"Welcome, American friends! Welcome!"* they chanted together.

A huge cheer rose in the distance.

"They're coming from the Bund." Third Sister sounded puzzled. She craned her neck toward the shouting.

"Can you see them?" Shao-shao asked, pulling at her skirt.

"No. I thought they'd come from the other way, through the British . . ."

Her words were lost as hundreds of voices shouted, "China Ten Thousand Years! America Ten Thousand Years!" Firecrackers exploded everywhere. Through the din, Shao-shao heard a horn tooting, an engine growling. He stepped into the street and stared straight at the nose of an approaching car. Shao-shao thought it looked like the face of a fantastic animal. The glittering round headlights would be the eyes and the chrome grille, gleaming in the sun,

193

was the mouth. The Chinese driver honked impatiently at the people who blocked his way.

Shao-shao stayed as close to the car as he could. Third Sister, hemmed in by the crowd behind him, could not pluck him back. The car's windows were rolled down, and an American leaned out, grinning and waving. He wore a white shirt, open at the collar, his sleeves rolled up. His fine fair hair was rumpled in the heat.

"Welcome!" Shao-shao cried, as the car came close, the shining black front fender almost grazing his thigh. *"Welcome, American friends!"* Cheers swelled from the crowd around him. He raised his arms over his head and waved both flags.

For one long moment, Shao-shao was face-to-face with the American. The smiling blue eyes looked directly into his. He looks like someone I saw in a movie, Shao-shao thought. The American spoke in English, and the car went on. He looked so happy, waving and smiling. He deserved to be happy. His country had won, had saved China.

Shao-shao felt a great bubble of excitement swell inside him. *"Welcome! Welcome!* America Ten Thousand Years!" he shouted after the car.

". . . never seen such a big car!"
". . . just like Jimmy Stewart!"
". . . says there are more coming!"
". . . Japs watched them pass, calm as can be!"
". . . smiled right at me."
Back in the family room, everyone shouted at once,

194

trying to tell Mother about the Americans. Shao-shao and Second Brother paid no attention to the knock at the door.

But Fourth Sister cried, "I'll go. It's probably Mei-ling."

Why is she so excited to have Mei-ling visit? Shao-shao wondered. She had just seen Mei-ling. Anyway, he couldn't understand why she would want to be friends with someone who had treated her so badly all summer.

The sound of a familiar voice pushed that thought out of his head.

Mother stood straight up, her cheeks white as chalk under her rouge. She put her hand out blindly, as if she was afraid she would fall, and found Shao-shao's shoulder.

"I'm not Second Brother!" Fourth Sister's voice, shrill with indignation and excitement, rose up the stairs.

"You sure fooled me! What happened to your hair?" Father's laugh seemed to shake the house.

Shao-shao started to run downstairs, then stopped, suddenly shy.

"Shao-shao." Mother's voice trembled. "Go down and tell Gao-ma to make some tea for your father. Now!" She pushed him toward the kitchen stairs.

From the kitchen, Shao-shao heard the sounds of footsteps on the stairs, heard the shuffle of feet as Second Brother and Third Sister went to greet Father. Gao-ma poured water from the black kettle into Father's porcelain mug, while Ah-fong fluttered about, too excited to do anything. Gao-ma set the mug on a tray, preparing to climb the stairs.

"Let me," Shao-shao begged.

"Good," said Gao-ma, giving him the tray. She thudded up the stairs ahead of him and opened the door to the family room. Gripping the tray, terrified he would drop it, Shao-shao did not take his eyes off it until he came to a stop in front of Father.

Father's hair looked grayer than Shao-shao remembered. He wore a wrinkled blue cotton gown, dusty and stained, and worn cloth shoes. His eyes were puffy with fatigue, and there were new lines around his mouth. He looked straight at Shao-shao's face and smiled tiredly.

"Shao-shao is here," he said, gently gripping Shao-shao's arms with his hands, as if he needed to keep his balance. "You've grown tall and good-looking."

"I brought tea for you, Father."

"Thank you. It's just what I wanted." Father took the tea and sat down.

Fourth Sister pulled Shao-shao's sleeve. "Father thought I was Second Brother." She giggled.

"Father." Third Sister reached out toward Father, though she was too far away to touch him. "Are we still going to Chungking?"

"No." Father smiled again, looking around as if he couldn't believe he was home. "No, everyone from Chungking's moving here." He looked up at Mother. "Ho Tei-wu and I are going back into the export business. Now that the war is over, everyone wants Chinese cloth. I can keep my government post, too.

So Third Sister can continue at St. John's."

Third Sister's face seemed to glow like a dragon's pearl. "I'll call First Sister," she said.

Mother did not answer. Shao-shao knew she was too happy to speak. He stepped back to stand beside her.

Father turned to Second Brother. "There will be a job for you until we have money enough to send you to college, and for your oldest brother, when he comes back. If we all help, we might make a fortune."

His words were bold, but his voice sounded weary. He's been afraid, too, Shao-shao thought. He had to cross battlefields to get home. He had to bribe the Japanese, and maybe even the Communist rebels. He's come a long way.

Father held out his empty cup. "Shao-shao, would you get me some more?" he asked. "You're lucky to be the youngest. By the time you're old enough to go to college, we should have money to send you abroad. Then your future really will be boundless."

Shao-shao couldn't imagine that. All he knew was that he must tell Father something, that very moment, before he got the tea.

"I'm glad you're home," he said.

Margaret Chang was born in California's High Sierra and grew up in postwar Los Angeles. Her two abiding interests as a child were reading and observing the marine life in the tidepools and on the beaches of Southern California. After graduating from library school in the East, where she specialized in service to children, she worked in the Lexington, Massachusetts, public schools and at the New York Public Library. Her marriage to Raymond Chang took her to Williamstown, Massachusetts, where she has lived ever since. In Williamstown, Margaret Chang has been a high-school librarian, mother, community volunteer, playwright, student and teacher of children's literature, and "constant scribbler."

Raymond Chang was born in Hong Kong, moved to Shanghai when he was very small, and lived in Shanghai during the 1940s, from the Japanese occupation through the Communist regime. He later graduated from the University of London with first-class honors in chemistry and earned a Ph.D. from Yale University. After brief stints as a postdoctoral researcher in St. Louis and as a teacher at Hunter College, Raymond Chang became a teacher of chemistry at Williams College in Williamstown, Massachusetts, where he has lived since 1968. For relaxation, he maintains a forest garden, plays tennis, and practices the violin.

EDUCATION

Date Due